Princess Before Dawn

A Tale of the Wide-Awake Princess

Princess
Before
Dawn

E. D. BAKER

BLOOMSBURY

NEW YORK   LONDON   OXFORD   NEW DELHI   SYDNEY

First published in the United States of America in March 2018
by Bloomsbury Children's Books
www.bloomsbury.com

Bloomsbury is a registered trademark of Bloomsbury Publishing Plc

For information about permission to reproduce selections from this book, write to Permissions, Bloomsbury Children's Books, 1385 Broadway, New York, New York 10018
Bloomsbury books may be purchased for business or promotional use. For information on bulk purchases please contact Macmillan Corporate and Premium Sales Department at specialmarkets@macmillan.com

Library of Congress Cataloging-in-Publication Data
Names: Baker, E. D., author.
Title: Princess before dawn / by E. D. Baker.
Description: New York : Bloomsbury, 2018. | Series: Wide-awake princess ; 7
Summary: Annie and Liam call on their friends Francis and Zoë to help when a strange group visits Treecrest and takes over the hunting grounds.
Identifiers: LCCN 2017024229 (print) • LCCN 2017038523 (e-book)
ISBN 978-1-68119-673-2 (hardcover) • ISBN 978-1-68119-674-9 (e-book)
Subjects: | CYAC: Fairy tales. | Princesses—Fiction. | Magic—Fiction. | Vampires—Fiction. | Characters in literature—Fiction.
Classification: LCC PZ8.B173 Prt 2018 (print) | LCC PZ8.B173 (e-book) | DDC [Fic]—dc23
LC record available at https://lccn.loc.gov/2017024229

Book design by Donna Mark
Typeset by Westchester Publishing Services
Printed and bound in the U.S.A. by Berryville Graphics Inc., Berryville, Virginia
2 4 6 8 10 9 7 5 3 1

All papers used by Bloomsbury Publishing, Inc., are natural, recyclable products made from wood grown in well-managed forests. The manufacturing processes conform to the environmental regulations of the country of origin.

This book is dedicated to Kim, who helps me in so
many ways, to Victoria, my guiding light, and to my
fans who have continued to ask about Zoë and Francis.

Princess Before Dawn

CHAPTER 1

TWO WEEKS HAD passed since Annie and Liam had returned the pearl to the sea monster. After coming home to Dorinocco, planning their coronation had taken up nearly all their time.

"I really wish you hadn't invited all the fairies from Treecrest *and* Dorinocco to the coronation," Liam told Annie as they ate their breakfast in the sunlit private dining room. "You know how much trouble fairies can make, and there will be so many of them!"

Edda, Annie's troll dog, looked up at her adoringly. The enormous dog had put her head in Annie's lap as soon as they sat down. Annie scratched Edda behind the ears, then slipped a piece of sausage to her. "They'd make even more trouble if I hadn't invited them. Remember what happened with our first wedding?" Annie said to Liam. "They ruined it when they thought we hadn't sent them invitations."

"Thanks to Squidge," Liam muttered as he reached for another pastry.

"Did someone call my name?" the little sprite said, appearing in the doorway.

Annie blinked in surprise as he stepped into the room and climbed onto an empty chair. "Did you show up because Liam said your name?" she asked.

Squidge chuckled. "Names are powerful things and you should never say them unless you're willing to face the consequences." He was grinning when he looked at Annie's and Liam's incredulous faces. When he opened his mouth again, he had a twinkle in his eyes, but he seemed to rethink whatever he was going to say and sighed instead. "I could tell you that Liam called me by saying my name—and I bet I could get you to believe it—but I promised the fairies that I'd behave. They are such spoilsports lately."

"What are you talking about?" asked Liam.

"The fairies actually sent me here to help you plan your coronation," the sprite explained. "They said I owed you community service and that I had to do whatever you wanted."

"And why should we trust you?" Liam asked, frowning.

"Because they said they'd turn me into a gnat if I made any more mischief. I hate gnats and they know it."

"What if we say we don't need your help?" Annie asked him.

2

Squidge shrugged. "Of course you need my help. I can do all sorts of things that you can't. I was very useful when I helped you get ready for your wedding. Remember how I washed all the dogs and scrubbed the dungeon steps and—"

"Didn't send out the invitations when you told us you had?" said Annie. "Yes, we remember."

"I won't sabotage it this time. I promise!" Squidge exclaimed. "Now tell me, what do you have planned so far?"

"Don't tell him," Liam said to Annie.

"I don't know if it matters," she replied. "He'd find out anyway. We're going to have a traditional ceremony, then the feast and coronation ball. We were just about to discuss the menu before you popped up."

"Good! I like talking about food, although I like eating it even more," Squidge said, eyeing the food on the table. "Can you pass me some of those pastries? I'm about to faint from hunger."

There was a knock on the door and a footman peeked in. "Your Majesties, a fairy just dropped off a message from the king and queen of Treecrest."

"What do you suppose your parents want?" Liam said to Annie. "We were there just a few weeks ago."

"I'll take it," Annie told the footman.

He hurried into the room and handed her a folded slip of parchment, then bowed and left.

"Oh, dear," Annie said when she'd read it. "This can't

be good. They said that they need our help and want us to come right away. It's an emergency. The castle is overrun with uninvited guests who refuse to leave."

"How is that an emergency?" asked Liam.

"I suppose that depends on the guests," said Annie. "I can get ready immediately, but we need to tell your father."

"I'm going, too!" Squidge cried as Annie and Liam stood.

Annie shook her head. "I don't think so. You haven't done anything to make me think we can trust you."

"What if I polish everyone's shoes?" said the sprite. "Or give you flowers every day? Or pick the fleas off all the dogs?"

"You could start by apologizing," Liam told him. "And then work at being good as hard as you worked at being bad."

"I'm sorry, I'm sorry, I'm sorry times a hundred billion, gajillion times!" Squidge cried, clasping his hands in front of him. "Will you ever forgive me?"

"Only if you truly behave yourself!" Annie warned him.

"I'll be as good as gold!" Squidge declared. "No, make that as good as a gooseberry pie! They're my favorite. But I should really have a few more of those pastries before I go anywhere."

꙰

"Uninvited guests?" King Montague said, rubbing his leg that was hurting from gout again. Annie and Liam had gone to see Liam's father to tell him that they would be away for a day or so. "That could mean anything from enemy soldiers at the gates to bedbugs in the linens. Neither one is good. Would you like me to send some knights with you just in case?"

"The message didn't say it was an invasion, so I don't think we'll need any knights," said Liam. "But thank you for the offer. Besides, Annie and I are traveling by postcard. We'll be in Treecrest moments after we leave here. Traveling with knights would take us too long. Whatever the problem is, we hope to settle it quickly and get back here as soon as possible. We've already told everyone what they need to do to prepare for the coronation."

"I'll make sure they keep working on it," his father replied. "And I'll keep Edda here with me. We get along just fine, don't we, girl?" Summoning the dog by patting his gouty leg, the king grimaced when it hurt.

Edda left Annie's side and lumbered over to sit beside Montague, who immediately started petting her.

"Is there anything else you need me to do?" he asked Annie and Liam.

"Just rest and take care of your leg. I'd like to dance with you at least once at the coronation ball," Annie said, and kissed him on the cheek before she left with Liam.

CHAPTER 2

"THIS SHOULD BE FUN!" Squidge exclaimed. "I've never traveled by postcard before. What do I have to do?"

Annie smiled at Liam. They had traveled by magic postcard so many times by now that it was no longer as exciting as it had been at first. Having someone with them who had never traveled that way before was fun, even if it was the annoying little sprite.

"Nothing," Annie said as she picked him up and reached for Liam's hand.

The sprite had joined them in the king's audience chamber just moments before. His pockets were bulging with pastries and he had icing on his chin and lips.

"I mean, should I hold my breath or close my eyes or stick my fingers in my nose and plug my ears or stand on my head and gargle or—"

Liam touched the postcard that he'd placed in his pocket. A moment later they were standing on the gravel road that led to the drawbridge, looking up at the castle where Annie had been born.

"Wow!" Squidge cried as Annie set him down. "That was fast! Can we do it again?"

"Not right now," Annie said, laughing. "It works only one way."

"We need to get more postcards. This sure beats tricking a rabbit into giving me a ride or calling up a wind to carry me. Say, I know that cat!" he said when he spotted a gray tabby at the edge of the moat. "Mind if I go say hello? I'll only be a minute. I'll see you later!"

The little sprite had run off to join his friend when something in the moat caught Annie's eye. "Do you see that?" she asked Liam, nudging him in the side. "There are people swimming in the moat!"

"Yuck! I'd never do that," Liam replied. "Granted, your moat is cleaner than most, but it's a long way from being safe enough to drink or to swim in. Who are those women?"

"No one from around here," Annie said, trying not to stare.

Four fully dressed women were swimming in the moat near the drawbridge. Their long hair streamed out behind them as they paddled from one side to the other, fouling the water with dirt and oil and turning it murky. The women were talking and laughing, their harsh cackles grating on Annie's nerves. "*These* must be the uninvited guests," she whispered to Liam.

"Watch out!" Liam cried, grabbing Annie's arm to stop her from walking into a man who had suddenly materialized in front of them. The man was shorter than Annie, and was wearing a bright blue cape over a dark blue tunic and leggings. He had stopped to tuck a magic postcard into a pocket when Annie almost stumbled to avoid him. The man barely spared them a glance over his shoulder as he headed to the drawbridge.

"I don't think those women are the only uninvited guests here today," Liam told Annie.

"It's those darn postcards!" Annie said as they followed the man to the castle courtyard. "I knew when I first saw them in the Magic Marketplace that they were going to create problems!"

Annie was already upset as they started across the drawbridge, but when she heard the ruckus and saw what lay beyond she was horrified. Strangers milled around the courtyard, getting in the way of the castle residents who were trying to go about their regular business. She saw a footman carrying a box unable to move because of the crowd around him. A stable boy couldn't reach the stable with the horse he was leading because of the people blocking him. Two knights trying to get to the guardhouse were stuck behind a group of wildly dressed men and women who were loudly criticizing the castle's architecture. These weren't the ordinary merchants who often came to the castle, nor

8

were they visitors from any of Treecrest's neighbors. When Annie saw one wave a wand and turn the dovecote into a giant beehive, she knew exactly what they were.

Witches had used the magic postcards to come to Treecrest.

"I think I understand the problem now," she said to Liam through gritted teeth. "Let's go inside."

It took a while for Annie and Liam to work their way across the courtyard to the castle steps. Every time they saw an opening in the crowd, someone else would step up to fill it. Annie tried to be polite at first, saying "excuse me" even when someone bumped into her, but she finally began to lose patience and started pushing between people as she'd seen the strangers do.

When Annie was born, the fairy Moonbeam had given her the gift that no magic could touch her. This also meant that anyone else's magic didn't work when Annie was nearby. Even being close to Annie could diminish magic, although the effect wasn't permanent. None of the witches and wizards seemed to notice that their appearance changed or their magic no longer worked when Annie touched them. Even if they had, she was soon lost in the crowd and they couldn't have guessed that she was the reason for the change.

Walking up the castle steps proved to be just as difficult as crossing the courtyard. One old woman was sitting on the steps, pointing a wand at the sky. When

Annie looked up, she saw pigeons flying in circles overhead, following the movement of the wand. Everyone had to work their way around the woman, who didn't seem to know or care that she was in the way. A few steps higher, a man was juggling balls of light. When he dropped one, it landed on another man's shoulder. Although the light sputtered and went out, the second man turned around and shoved the juggler. Liam grabbed hold of Annie and dragged her through the crowd as the men started to fight, tossing spiders and sparks at each other.

The corridor inside wasn't quite as crowded, and Annie and Liam were able to make their way to the great hall without too much trouble. A statue of Captain Sterling, the captain of the guard, stood just inside the door. The statues of two of his men stood beside him. Someone had painted all three in bright splashes of blues, purples, and yellows, while someone else had wrapped the scarf from a lady's hat around the statue of the captain. Peeking around the statues, Annie saw that there appeared to be a party going on with a table set up for food at one end and a large group dancing to fiddle music in the middle. Witches and wizards stood in small groups, comparing notes on magic.

A witch standing by herself was popping bright red beans into her mouth, chewing them, then spitting them into a silver cup that Annie recognized as belonging to the royal family. The scent of something spicy was almost overwhelming when the witch opened her mouth, flashing teeth and gums as red as blood. As soon as the cup was full, the witch swirled its contents, muttered a few words, and poured it on the floor. The scarlet pulp turned into salamanders that scuttled off into the rushes.

"Look at all the food on that table!" Liam said as they made their way into the room. "It's enough to feed everyone in the entire castle for days! Do you suppose the cook made it or these people used a magic tablecloth like the animals from Brementown gave to Gwennie?"

"Good question," Annie said, shaking her head. The witches and wizards were gathered around the table as they picked at the roast boar, stuffed peacock, beef haunch, huge platter of fish, and mountain of pastries. Squidge and the gray tabby were there, too, helping themselves from the platters.

Annie and Liam were crossing the room when suddenly Liam began to dance to the music of the fiddle. "What are you doing?" Annie asked, surprised.

Liam looked confused as he exclaimed, "I don't know, but I can't help it!"

Annie glanced at the other people who were all dancing in the same way. Most of them had their backs to her as they faced the fiddle, but she thought one of them might work in the kitchen. The only person who seemed to be enjoying herself was the witch playing

11

the fiddle. While Annie watched, the witch headed to the food-laden table while the fiddle hung in the air, still playing where she'd left it.

"Let's get out of here," Annie said, touching Liam's back.

As soon as the magic no longer controlled him, he stopped dancing with a sigh of relief and joined her as she headed for the door. "Thank you," he said. "I've never really liked dancing, especially like that."

"You're very welcome!" Annie told him with a smile. "I wonder how long those people have been dancing. The ones I saw looked awfully tired. Do you mind if we go to the kitchen? I want to see if Cook is making all that food. If she is, she'll use up all the stores and the buttery will be empty in days."

"Lead on," Liam said. "I'm curious, too."

Although they didn't hear the usual bustle and clang coming from the kitchen, they did hear two voices. When they peeked inside, neither Cook nor any of her helpers were there. Instead, two witches were stirring something that smelled like rancid fat in Cook's biggest pot while they compared recipes.

"I use the hair of the dog that bit me and the rag-weed that made me sneeze instead of henbane and bat ears," one witch said. "I find that personalizing a potion like that works better."

The second witch was mumbling something when Annie spotted Squidge in the corner, sharing a hunk of cheese with the gray tabby cat. The little sprite saw them and waved, but the cat didn't even look up.

"I've seen more than enough," Annie told Liam. "It's time we found my parents. I think I know what I have to do, but I want to talk to them first."

❧

They located Annie's parents in her father's chamber behind a locked and barricaded door. Annie had to assure them that she and Liam were alone before a footman would let them in. Once Annie and Liam were in the room, the servants locked the door and pushed a heavy table in front of it. Annie was surprised by how many people were there. All of her mother's ladies-in-waiting were crowded into the two rooms along with her father's attendants, half the guards, and at least a dozen servants.

"We thought everyone would be safer here with us than downstairs with those horrible people," the queen said when she saw Annie looking around in surprise.

"You do realize that 'those people' are witches and can probably go anywhere they want, right?" said Annie.

"I know, but we were hoping they'd leave us alone if they had the run of the rest of the castle," the queen replied.

Annie glanced at Liam. Her parents must be truly frightened to have given up the castle to strangers.

13

"I'm just glad that you and Liam got here safely," said the king. "We asked Captain Sterling to make the witches leave, but you saw what they did to him. Anyone who goes near the great hall now gets dragged into their dance. We didn't know what to do, so we sent for you hoping that you might have an idea. Your mother thought it best that we stay in my chambers until you arrived."

Annie nodded. "I wondered about those statues. Those poor men!"

"When did your 'uninvited guests' start arriving?" asked Liam.

"Yesterday morning," the queen told him. "It was just a few at first, but then one of them left and a few minutes later returned with a huge crowd. More have been coming ever since. We didn't know they were magic users until that horrible woman pointed her finger at the captain and his men, turning them to stone."

"And then that other witch made the scullery girls start dancing," added the king.

"They're still dancing," said Liam. "We saw them just a bit ago."

"The newcomers all looked like strangers," said Annie. "Am I right in saying that none of them came from around here?"

"As far as we know," said the queen. "No one in the castle recognized them. All these awful people in my

14

castle! I don't know what we're going to do to make them leave."

"I do," Annie said, and headed for the door. "Let me out and barricade the door again. The party is over and it's time for those guests to go home."

"You're not going out there by yourself!" said Liam.

"Why not? They can't hurt me with their magic," Annie told him.

"Not directly, but if they use their magic on something else, it could hurt you," Liam replied. "Remember how Terobella sent the crows to hurt you and how she made the bridge collapse under your carriage? If you're leaving this room, I'm going with you."

"And you say I'm stubborn!" said Annie. "All right, but you have to let me do the talking."

⁂

When Annie and Liam returned to the great hall, the witches and wizards seemed even rowdier than before. A witch had discovered an empty suit of armor and was making it walk around, banging into things. She had also made two antique swords come down from the wall to fight each other. Annie recognized them; one had belonged to her grandfather and one to her great-grandfather. For as long as she could remember, no one had been allowed to touch them, let alone use them in a fight.

The wizard Annie and Liam had followed across the drawbridge had come inside and was holding court at the far end of the hall. His cape was thrown back and he was talking in a loud voice, telling those gathered around him that he was the personal friend of a dragon that had given him a scale to enhance his magic.

"Is that so?" said another wizard. "Prove it, you old windbag!"

The wizard dressed in blue looked down his nose at the other man and said in a haughty voice, "I don't need to prove anything to you, but I will show my friends." Reaching into a fold in his cape, he took out something no bigger than a goose egg and held it up for all to see. Annie knew some actual dragons. If this was a real dragon's scale, it was so small and chipped that it must have been an old one that fell off an undersized dragon.

The witch with the fiddle changed her tune just then, drawing Annie's gaze to the dancers. They looked as if they were ready to collapse and she was sorry that she hadn't done something to help them sooner.

"May I have your attention, please!" Annie called out, but the noise in the hall was too loud and no one paid her any attention.

Annie glanced around the room. The noisiest thing there was the fiddle. If she could silence it, she was sure to get the attention of some of the witches. "Stay here," she told Liam, and started toward the witch with the instrument.

The woman had her back turned when Annie reached out and snatched the fiddle from her. Three notes sounded, each one fainter than the last. When it finally went silent, everyone in the hall turned to look at her. Annie's plan had worked better than she'd hoped.

"What did you just do?" the witch screamed at Annie. "You broke my fiddle!"

"I didn't break it," Annie told her. "I just took away its magic."

"You can't do that! No one can!" the witch scoffed.

"You don't know who I am, do you? I'm Princess Annabelle. I've been away, but I'm home now. I have one magical gift, which is that magic doesn't work around me. Let me show you," Annie said, and placed her hand on the witch's arm.

"Get away from me!" the woman cried, and pointed her finger at Annie. "You're just a flea!" When nothing happened, the witch studied her finger as if it were faulty. When she looked at Annie again, her eyes grew big and she backed away. "You took my magic!"

"I did," said Annie as she started walking around the hall. "And you're only the beginning."

One after another, Annie touched the strangers. Wands flashed or sparked or shot bolts of light as some of the witches and wizards tried to stop her before she could reach them, but the magic rebounded and they fell prey to their own spells. Annie spotted a dust pan, a chicken, two frogs, and a pig where some of the magic users had been standing. When Annie touched the woman who'd been playing with the suit of armor, the armor and the two swords fell to the floor with a clatter. Whimpering, the woman reached into her pocket and drew out her magic postcard. A moment later she was gone.

Turning to the witch who still had red teeth and gums, Annie touched her hand while grabbing the silver cup from her grasp. The witch was crying when she took hold of her magic postcard and disappeared.

Witches and wizards began disappearing left and right, although a few ran from the hall to warn others. Soon only the wizard who had been bragging about his friendship with a dragon was left standing at the far end of the room. Holding the scale in one hand, he muttered something and waved his other hand at a mouse scurrying across the floor. The mouse grew and grew until it was the size of a lion. Liam jumped between Annie and the giant mouse, brandishing his sword. When the beast gnashed its teeth and lunged at Liam, Annie noticed that the man's lips were still moving, and all his concentration was on the fight.

Still watching the wizard, Annie walked to the wall and crept the length of the room until she was behind him. He was shouting encouragement to his giant mouse when Annie reached out and touched the man. The mouse shrank with a small pop and scurried away.

Liam completed his last lunge, tripping when there was nothing in front of him.

"How dare you?" the wizard shouted at Annie.

Strangers wouldn't know that her ability to negate magic worked only when she was touching them; Annie didn't want them to stick around long enough to find out.

"This is my castle," said Annie. "Magic like yours isn't welcome here and neither are you. Leave and don't ever come back or you'll lose your magic for good!"

Panicked, the wizard touched his magic postcard and disappeared.

"Thank you!" said a voice as Annie turned to find Captain Sterling at her side, no longer a statue yet still covered with splotches of paint.

"Are you all right?" she asked him.

Captain Sterling nodded. "I'm fine, thanks to you. But it looks as if those nasty people used real paint on me, and not something they conjured up with magic. I hope it comes off with soap and water."

"I'm so sorry about that," said Annie. "It might not have happened if I had come sooner."

The captain shrugged. "It's fine," he said. "After all, I'd much rather deal with a little paint than be a statue any day."

CHAPTER 3

ANNIE AND LIAM SEARCHED the hallways to make sure that none of the witches and wizards had stayed behind. Most of them were gone, but the few that Annie found hiding out disappeared in a hurry once they saw what would happen if she touched them. The uninvited guests had made a huge mess in the great hall and the courtyard. When the people who lived in the castle emerged, they were dismayed at what they saw, but it didn't take long for them to start cleaning.

While servants bustled around her, Annie searched for any remnants of magic in the great hall. She found a silver slipper that turned into a smelly old shoe when she touched it, a sparkling hair comb that turned to wood, and half a dozen salamanders hiding in the rushes. The salamanders stained her fingers red when they turned back into bean pulp. Squidge helped by catching and eating a salamander that was too quick for Annie.

"What happened to you?" the queen asked when she came down to survey the damage to the castle. "Are you bleeding?"

Annie glanced at her hands. "No, it was the salamanders," she said. "I hope this washes off."

The queen looked confused, but all she said was, "I worry about you. How have you been?"

"Great," Annie replied. "Liam and I have been getting ready for his coronation."

"It's your coronation as well," her mother reminded her. "You'll be queen of Dorinocco. I'm glad you won't have to deal with that awful Lenore or Liam's terrible brother, Clarence."

Liam's mother and brother had sent a tiny spinning wheel to the castle so that Annie's sister, Gwendolyn, would touch it, making an evil fairy's curse come true. Annie had been the only one in the castle who hadn't fallen asleep, so it had been up to her to break the spell. The queen of Dorinocco and her awful son hadn't given up trying to take over Treecrest until Annie and Liam took them far away to live in exile.

Annie laughed. "So am I. We've already visited Liam's mother on the witch's island to take the bacon we'd promised. She seems to have made friends with some of the witches. I think she's happy there, although

I'm sure she'd never admit it. I have no idea how Clarence is doing, but he can't do too much damage in the jungle. As long as he stays far away, Liam and I will be happy."

"I know you're busy in your new home, but it would be nice if you could stay a few days," said the queen. "Your father and I miss you."

Annie glanced at Liam, who was helping put the antique swords back on the wall. "We'll stay until tomorrow at least. There's still a lot to do here."

"Good!" said the queen. "Your father will be so pleased. He likes company, just not the uninvited kind."

❧

Everyone was so busy putting the castle back in order that hours passed before Annie had the chance to talk to Liam again. They waved at each other in passing, but Annie could tell that he enjoyed being useful and she was determined to find every bit of wayward magic.

Annie was checking the last corner of the great hall when she found a long, golden staff. The moment she touched it, the staff turned into an ordinary cornstalk. She was carrying it outside when she stopped, stunned, as two centaurs trotted across the drawbridge. The centaur with flowing black hair and the body of a dun stallion whinnied. When an answering whinny came from the stable, both centaurs headed that way. Annie

22

noticed that the chestnut-colored centaur had a post-card in his hand.

"I don't think I should handle that one," Annie said, and called to a girl sweeping the steps. "Please tell Captain Sterling that two centaurs just arrived and are visiting the stable."

The girl nodded. "I'll tell him, but he's trying to get some water nymphs out of the moat."

That made Annie curious. "Never mind. I'll tell him myself," she said.

Hurrying down the steps, Annie detoured to a refuse pile to toss the cornstalk before heading across the drawbridge. A half dozen guards were watching two nymphs paddling in the moat. Captain Sterling looked unhappy and frustrated.

"But you can't stay here, ladies," he told the nymphs as Annie walked up.

"Every body of water needs a nymph to take care of it," the nymph with deep blue hair told him.

"Every *natural* body of water, perhaps," said Annie. "But this moat was dug many years ago. If you want a natural river, swim to the back of the castle, where the moat flows into the Crystal River."

"A river!" the nymphs squealed. Turning as one, they dove into the water and disappeared.

Annie told the captain about the centaurs in the stable and was about to go back inside the castle when she happened to see two short men approaching. One was tucking a postcard into the pocket of his brightly colored vest. The other was looking directly at her. "Captain," Annie said in a quiet voice. "I think we have more visitors."

Captain Sterling stood by her side as the men approached. When they drew closer, Annie realized that they weren't men at all, at least not the kind she was used to seeing. Neither one was over three feet tall, but that wasn't what made up her mind. Their heads and faces were too lumpy, their hands and feet too large, and they had identical bowed legs and humps in their backs. "What are they?" she whispered to the captain.

"Gnomes, maybe," he whispered in reply. "But I've only seen pictures, so I can't be sure."

"Hello!" said the older of the two. "We're strangers to these parts, and we were wondering if you could point the way to the nearest mountains."

"Go due north," said Annie, gesturing.

"Very good!" declared the other gnome. "Thank you, young lady."

Annie and the captain watched as the two figures headed up the road. "I wonder how many postcard holders have come by and not stopped at the castle," said Annie.

The captain shook his head. "There's no way to tell, but the only ones that concern me are the ones who come inside uninvited. Speaking of which, I need to go see about those centaurs. They must have gotten past the guards when those nymphs were here."

"And I have to finish checking the great hall," said Annie. "Although I think I'm almost finished."

๛

When Annie returned to the hall, the servants had finished cleaning it. However, Cook and all her helpers were scouring everything in the kitchen, so there was no midday meal. Instead the royal family ate an early supper a few hours later, although it was a simple feast of cured ham, beets, and turnips.

"I should be grateful that the witches just took food and didn't get into the treasury or the armory," said King Halbert. "We would have been in real trouble then. As it is, the steward assures me that Cook will be serving normal meals by tomorrow."

"Good!" Squidge said from under the table, where he was playing with the hounds. "I'll starve without my yummy stuff!"

"I just wish those witches didn't still have their postcards," Annie told them. "I don't like the idea that they could come back."

"I don't think they will as long as they think you're here," Liam replied. "They looked terrified when they left. I think they're more protective of their magic than even the vainest princess is of her beauty."

"From what I saw, some of the witches were

terrifying, although a few were very funny," said the queen. "I saw one who was dressed all in feathers; her gown and shoes were made of feathers, and she had some stuck in her hair. She even had live birds sitting on her shoulders!"

"Were they crows?" asked Liam.

The queen shook her head. "No, I think they were goldfinches. She chirped to them and they chirped back."

"I saw a water witch," said the king. "At least that's what I would have called her. She was dressed all in blue and she squelched when she walked as if her shoes were wet. When she aimed her wand, water shot out of it. She could write with the water and make pictures in the air. I thought she was entertaining until she shot water at one of my hounds and chased him from the hall." The king glanced at the hounds under the table and shook his head. "Dash still isn't with the others. I wonder where he is."

"I'll go look," Squidge cried, and scurried out from under the table.

"I'm surprised you brought that sprite with you after all the trouble he caused," the queen said to Annie.

Annie shrugged. "I believe in second chances. And he did apologize a hundred gajillion times and promise to be helpful."

"Hmm," said the king. "We'll see."

26

"You never did tell me how your hands got red, Annie," said the queen.

Annie told her about the witch chewing beans and using the pulp to make salamanders. When the servants came in to light the torches on the walls, the family was still talking about the other odd things they'd seen. Annie glanced at the windows set high in the wall and saw that it was getting dark out. "I didn't realize that we'd been sitting here so long."

"Neither did I," her mother said. "I believe an early night is in order, considering the day we've had." When she stood, everyone else did, too. "Good night, my dears. Thank you for coming so quickly and helping us with those people."

"That's what family does," Annie replied.

ॐ

Only a short time later, Annie and Liam were walking down the corridor when they heard a dog barking and Squidge shouting, "Whoa, boy!"

"That doesn't sound good," Liam said, and they started to run. They found the sprite seated on Dash's back while the hound barked and threw himself at the door to the cellar. Squidge clung to the collar, yanking it as if he was trying to rein in a horse.

"What is Dash barking at?" Annie asked the sprite.

"I don't know," Squidge replied. "I was riding him to

27

the great hall when he smelled something and went crazy."

"Maybe he smells rats," Annie said to Liam. "Remember how many ran up the stairs when the cellar flooded?"

"It's not rats," shouted the sprite as the barking grew louder. "I can smell it, too."

"Then what is it?" Liam said as guards arrived to see what all the commotion was about.

Two guards took up positions on either side of Liam while a third pulled the hound away from the door. Everyone else stood back as Liam jerked the door open. At first, there was nothing to see in the darkness of the stairwell, but after a few moments, shadows began to shift and gather at the bottom of the stairs. There was a whisper of sound and one of the shadows detached itself from the others and started up the steps. Liam and the guards backed away as a tall, thin man dressed all in black entered the light of the torches.

"Good evening," he said with a strange accent. "I am the Duke of Highcliff. It is good to finally meet the owners of this castle."

"I'm not the owner," said Liam. "This castle belongs to King Halbert and Queen Karolina. What were you doing in the cellar?"

"Resting until it was time for the festivities to begin," said the duke. "My friends and I would like to thank the owners for their hospitality. Their cellar is most peaceful and delightfully dark. No sunlight penetrated to disturb our sleep."

"You were down there all day?" asked Annie. She was bursting with questions, but just then a large group of people started up the stairs, nodding to Annie and Liam as they pushed past into the corridor, one after the other. Dismayed, Annie watched as they filed into the great hall. Nearly every one of these new, uninvited guests, was well groomed and dressed, although their clothing styles varied and were quite different from those in Treecrest or Dorinocco. High collars and formfitting clothes seemed to be most common, but they were all made of costly fabrics and furs, and their shoes were of the finest leather. They were either nobility or very rich, and they all acted as if they had every right to be there. The only ones who didn't look wealthy were carrying musical instruments.

Annie studied the last people to leave the cellar. Unlike the witches who looked like normal people in strange clothing, these people looked a little off, although she couldn't tell how at first. It wasn't until she looked at the duke again that she noticed how he and his friends were different from most people. Every one of them had pale skin and piercing eyes. They also seemed to have too many teeth in their mouths, or at least teeth that were bigger and longer than normal. She noticed their scent, as well. Although some had doused themselves heavily with perfume, nothing could cover up the musky, sour scent that still clung to them.

A man dressed like the duke stopped to talk to him. He looked a lot like the Duke of Highcliff, although not quite so tall or so thin, and his hair was two shades lighter.

"My nephew, Reynard," the duke told Annie and Liam.

Reynard turned to eye the young couple. Instead of talking to them, he turned back to the duke and said, "We won't start without you." When he walked away, Annie was struck by the way he moved, appearing to glide more than walk.

"When did you get here?" Liam asked the duke.

"We arrived shortly before dawn and postponed our ball until tonight."

"But no one invited you into the castle. You don't have any right to be here!" said Liam.

"Ah, but someone did invite us in," the duke replied. "I believe it was a woman dressed all in feathers. She arrived only moments after I did and was crossing the drawbridge when I asked if we might join her. She replied, 'Help yourself!' so we all came in."

Chords were struck in the great hall, and the musicians began to warm up. "Please excuse me," said the duke. "It seems our musicians are eager to begin."

Annie watched, dumbfounded, as the duke followed the last stragglers into the hall. "Is this really happening?" she asked Liam.

"I figured out what they smell like," Squidge said, tugging on the hem of Annie's gown. "They smell like pickled, dead squirrels. Just looking at them gives me the heebie-jeebies."

"I want to know who they are," said Liam. "I've never seen anyone like them before. Who sleeps in a cellar all day?"

"I don't like this one bit!" Annie told him.

"Let's see what they're doing," Liam suggested.

Gesturing to the guards to accompany them, Annie, Liam, and Squidge returned to the doorway into the great hall and looked inside. The musicians had taken up a position at the far end of the hall, while the other strangers had chosen partners and were swooping and twirling from one end to the other. The servants who had been cleaning up after the evening meal stood against the wall, looking confused. Annie noticed that one of the servers was nearby. Thinking about the way Captain Sterling had been turned into a statue, she hurried to the girl's side and whispered, "Please tell all our people to leave the hall. I don't want anything bad to happen to them."

While the girl spread the word, Annie returned to Liam. "They're very energetic dancers," he said, watching the uninvited guests. "That's a strenuous dance, but none of them seem to be tiring."

"At least they're not raiding the kitchen," said Annie. "Or taking things down from the walls."

"Yet," Liam muttered. "Their ball has only just begun."

Squidge scrunched his face and shook his head. "I don't like them. I thought the witches were kind of fun, but there's something about these people I really don't like. I just don't know what it is yet."

Although Annie and Liam stayed to watch from the doorway, the dancers never seemed to tire, nor did they leave the room for any reason. "It looks as if they could keep this up all night," Annie finally said. "I'd like to let my father get a good night's sleep, but I think we really should tell him about this."

Liam nodded. "The guards can take shifts watching the guests. Let's just hope these people are gone in the morning."

"I'll watch them, too," said Squidge. "I don't trust them any more than I would a flea on my own backside."

After talking to the guards, Annie and Liam hurried up the stairs. Her father's attendant protested that the king was asleep when Annie knocked on the door to his bedchamber and walked in.

"I'm sorry to wake you, but we have another group of uninvited guests," Annie told the king as he sat up, looking groggy. "Apparently they spent the day in the cellar and came out after dark."

The king looked fully awake as he pulled back the covers and stood up. "Tell me everything you can about them."

Liam did most of the talking and described everything that they had seen. Annie added a few details, but they were both adamant that the king didn't need to go see them for himself, at least not yet. "We told the guards to watch them and let us know if anything happens. So far they haven't done anything but dance to the music of their own musicians."

"And you say they're not witches or wizards?" said the king.

Annie shook her head. "We watched them for a while and I didn't sense any use of magic."

"Then let them dance," the king told them. "We'll deal with them in the morning."

CHAPTER 4

WORRIED ABOUT WHAT THEIR newest guests might be doing, Annie and Liam were up early the next morning. They had almost reached the great hall and were talking about how quiet it was when Ewan, the page, stopped them.

"Their Majesties King Halbert and Queen Karolina request that you join them in the queen's solarium."

"I didn't think they'd be up this early," Annie said to Liam.

"Do you know if Captain Sterling has gone to see them yet today?" Liam asked the page.

"He's with them now," Ewan replied.

Anxious to hear what the captain had to report, Annie and Liam hurried to the solarium. They found the captain and Squidge there, still talking to Annie's parents. Everyone looked up when Annie and Liam walked into the room.

"The captain was just telling us about our newest guests," said King Halbert. "Captain Sterling, please continue."

"I told Their Majesties that the 'guests' danced until just before dawn, then returned to the cellar," said the captain. "We haven't heard a sound from them since."

"I did," said Squidge. "My hearing is lots better than yours. Right after they went down there, I heard a tapping sound like a bunch of people were walking on stone, then a whooshy sort of sound. *Then* it got real quiet."

There was a knock on the door, which opened to admit the elderly guard Horace. His face was flushed and he was out of breath from running. "Your Majesties, Captain Sterling, two of the guards have been found unconscious."

"Which guards?" asked Captain Sterling. "Were they injured?"

"Halstead and Wallace," Horace told him. "A scullery maid found them. They were watching the dancing in the great hall for half the night, but they disappeared after they went off duty. No one saw them again until the girl found them in the storage room next to the buttery a few minutes ago. We didn't want to move either one until you'd been down to see them."

"Take me to them," ordered the captain.

"I want to see them, too," Liam declared.

"If you'll excuse us?" Annie said to her parents.

"Go, then come back and tell us what you saw," said the king.

Squidge ran ahead while Annie and Liam followed Captain Sterling downstairs to the storage room. The cooks' helpers had gathered around the doorway, peering at the two men lying inside. "Everyone, get back to work," said the captain, and they all hurried off.

"These men are unusually pale," Liam said as he knelt beside the guard named Halstead.

Captain Sterling knelt beside Wallace. "I don't see a mark on them."

"Wait a moment...I see something," said Annie. "Look at their necks. Are those puncture wounds?"

Liam turned Halstead's head, exposing more of his neck. Two holes about an inch apart appeared bright red against the man's pale skin.

"Is that a snake bite?" asked Liam.

"Maybe a spider did it," said Squidge.

"Look, Wallace has the same bite on his neck."

"I've never seen anything like this," said Liam. "Why would this happen now? Do you think those people brought snakes or spiders into the castle?"

"This whole thing is so odd," said Annie. "Why would any creature bite two people in an identical place?"

"None of this makes sense," Liam told them.

"I'll send for a healer to look at them," said the

captain. "In the meantime, my men can take them to their quarters."

"And I'll go tell my parents what's going on," said Annie. "I'll be back as soon as I can."

The king and queen looked worried when Annie told them what she'd seen. "I suppose it could be spiders or snakes," said the queen. "But do you think you might have missed some of those salamanders that you told us about? Is it possible that some might have gotten away and are spreading through the castle, biting people?"

"Salamanders are very shy and wouldn't leave marks like that," said Annie. "I'm sure it wasn't a salamander."

"Ordinary salamanders might not bite like that, but a salamander that a witch created might be very different," said the queen.

"I really think I got them all," Annie told her.

"Either way, I'm ordering that all the rushes used to cover the castle floors be thrown out and replaced and that every able-bodied person start hunting for snakes, spiders, and anything else that doesn't belong here," said the king. "I want whatever bit those men to be out of here before nightfall!"

Annie left the room even more worried than she'd been before. She doubted very much that a snake or spider had been responsible, and feared that whatever had attacked them was something much worse. If her parents focused on the easy answer, they might completely overlook the real culprit. Although Annie thought that the answer might lie with the new uninvited visitors, she doubted that it was anything they had brought with them. Something her friend Millie had told her was nagging her. Although she hoped she was wrong, she had a sinking feeling that she knew what had bitten the two men.

When Annie returned downstairs to learn if there was any more news, Liam was still consulting with Captain Sterling while a group of guards stood by, waiting for orders. "Has anyone talked to the guests?" she asked the captain.

"No," said the captain. "It's a good idea. I'll go talk to them now. Horace, you're with me."

"Liam and I are going, too," Annie told him. "Those people are very odd. I'd like to learn more about them, if I can."

"Fine," said Liam. "But you stay behind us. We might be walking into a whole nest of snakes."

"Or spiders," Horace said, shuddering.

While Captain Sterling, Liam, and Squidge led the way, Annie followed with Horace. She had a feeling that the old man was determined to protect her, just as he'd tried so many times before. The men who were guarding the cellar door handed them torches, then watched from the top of the stairs as the small party warily took one step at a time.

After the fairies' rainstorm had flooded the cellar, they'd used their magic to dry it, but marks on the walls still showed just how high the water had risen. Aside from the empty barrels waiting to hold the fall harvest, the dirt floor was bare. Annie wondered why anyone would choose to sleep in a cellar, let alone one with no furniture.

"Be really quiet," whispered Squidge. "I have a bad feeling about this place."

"It's just a cellar," Annie whispered back.

"Then what's that?" Squidge asked, kicking the dirt to reveal a dry, shriveled object.

"An old turnip from last year," Annie told him.

"Oh, good!" replied the sprite, who picked it up and ate it.

Going from one small room to the next, the search party didn't see a single person.

"Where did they go?" asked Liam. "Do you think they used their postcards to return home?"

"It looks that way," said Annie.

"Then how come I can still smell them?" asked Squidge. "Unless they were so stinky that their smell stays around even after they're gone."

When a tiny movement above her caught Annie's eye, she held her torch high to get a better look. She gasped when she saw that the ceiling was covered with

39

bats hanging upside down from the uneven surface. Some seemed to be watching the search party, but the rest were asleep.

"Where did they come from?" said Annie. "Liam, do you think these could be the bats that the fairies brought here when they were trying to ruin our wedding?" She doubted it, but it would be a simpler answer, and one that wasn't nearly as awful as the possibility that seemed more and more likely.

"Maybe," said Liam. "Although I thought the fairies sent all the bats and squirrels back to the forest. And these bats look different. See, their faces aren't the same and their color is different."

Annie nodded when she took another look. These weren't the cute bats they'd seen before. Instead, these bats had split noses and sharp, protruding fangs. She thought they looked nasty and not at all friendly.

"Could these bats have bitten the men?" asked Horace.

"I wouldn't be surprised," said Liam. "Come on, let's get out of here until we decide how we'll deal with them."

"Princess, why don't you—" Horace began as he turned around. He wasn't looking where he was going when he bumped into an empty barrel, knocking it over with a crash and sending it careening across the floor.

"I told you to be quiet!" shouted Squidge.

Startled, the bats descended on the humans in a cloud of beating wings. Squidge darted up the stairs, shrieking the entire way. Annie covered her head with one arm while holding her torch high with the other. The men waved their torches in the air, trying to fend off the bats. Annie's head was down when Liam grabbed her arm and shuffled her across the cellar floor and up the stairs. Horace and the captain followed, holding the bats at bay with their fire.

When everyone was upstairs, Captain Sterling slammed the door shut. "I wish I'd had my sword with me," he said, looking grim. "I could have dispatched a good number of those filthy creatures."

"I wish I owned a sword," Squidge said. "Can you imagine how dashing I'd look?"

"That was horrible!" Annie exclaimed as she handed her torch to one of the guards. "How will we get rid of them?"

"I don't know," said the captain. "I suppose we could smoke them out."

Annie shook her head. "And fill the whole castle with suffocating fumes? My parents will never agree to that."

"I'll go talk to Their Majesties now," Captain Sterling declared.

"And I'll talk to some people who have dealt with bats," Liam told him. "I'm sure we'll come up with something."

41

"I'll ask the cat if he wants to go get something to drink with me," said Squidge. "That turnip made me thirsty."

Annie gave the sprite an annoyed glance before turning to Liam. "I'm going to do some research of my own. I'll be in my father's private meeting room if you need me."

While Liam and Captain Sterling were going to focus on getting rid of the bats, Annie had already decided to find out what she could about the people who had gone into the cellar. Millie had told her about her friend who claimed to be a vampire, something that didn't exist in Treecrest or the neighboring king-doms. But will-o'-the-wisps and dragons existed on the other side of the world when there was nothing like them here. Couldn't vampires be just as real? After talking to Millie, Annie had found her father's mythol-ogy book, the only place she had ever seen the word "vampire" mentioned. She remembered most of what she'd read, but not everything. It was time to refresh her memory.

Once she reached her father's meeting room, it didn't take her long to find the right book and carry it over to the big table in front of her father's chair. Annie flipped through the pages looking for the right section. Her dread mounted as she read the entry. According to the book, vampires slept during the day because of sunlight's deadly effect on them. They were generally very pale and had two long canine teeth, or fangs, with which they bit their victims' necks. They were also very strong and could easily overpower a grown man. The part that Annie found most interesting was the very last paragraph, which claimed that vampires could turn into bats.

"And we have a cellar full of them!" Annie said out loud.

Although the book didn't say anything about how to get rid of vampires, Annie already knew how she could find out. What better way to learn about vampires than to talk to one who would answer her questions? Regardless of what was happening in the castle, Annie had to go to Greater Greensward to meet Millie's friend, and she had to do it soon.

CHAPTER 5

ANNIE WAS EXCITED about going to Greater Greensward, not only because she hoped someone there could help them, but also to see her friends Millie and Audun. Annie and Liam had met the couple while on their grand tour. One of the postcards that Holly, the woods witch, had given them took them directly to the castle of Greater Greensward. They had met Millie and Audun only minutes after arriving, and had become friends while dealing with the nasty wizard Rotan. The only reason Annie and Liam had been able to return home when they did was because their new friends had taken them to the Magic Marketplace to purchase more postcards.

Now that Annie had a pressing reason, she couldn't wait to go back. After returning the book to the shelf, she started searching for Liam, but he wasn't in the great hall or anywhere else she looked. She found

Squidge peering into a mousehole with the cat, but when she asked if he'd seen Liam, he shrugged and said, "No, I've been too busy."

Finally spotting Captain Sterling in the corridor, Annie stopped him to ask, "Do you know where I can find Liam?"

The captain shook his head. "He left the castle a while ago to look for someone who knows about bats. I have no idea where he ended up going."

Annie was impatient to get started, but there was no way to predict when Liam would return. "I guess I have to go by myself," she murmured as she walked away.

Annie was thinking about everything she needed to do as she hurried upstairs to the chamber she shared with Liam. Opening the trunk where he kept his clothes, she took out the postcards and riffled through them until she found the cards for Greater Greensward and Treecrest. After tucking the Treecrest card in her pocket, she wrote a quick note to Liam, telling him where she was going and that she'd be back soon, then placed the note on his pillow, where he'd be sure to see it. When she was ready, she held the card for Greater Greensward in one hand and touched the center of the card with the other. A moment later, she was standing in front of the Greater Greensward castle.

The gray stone towers and the castle moat looked close enough to those in Treecrest that it all felt familiar, even though she'd visited Greater Greensward only once before. When she crossed the drawbridge, she half expected to see Liam or the captain. What she didn't expect was an adorable brown-and-white puppy that darted up and jumped against her legs, barking and wagging his tail.

"Why, hello there!" Annie said, bending down to pet the puppy. When she scratched behind his long, floppy ears, his entire body wriggled with joy.

"Felix!" a woman called from the top of the castle steps.

The puppy took off running, disappearing behind the stables. Annie turned toward the woman who reminded her of Millie. Although the woman had auburn hair and Millie's hair was blond, their faces were very similar. "I can help you catch the puppy if you'd like," Annie told her.

The woman laughed. "That puppy is actually my three-year-old son, Felix. He was just a baby when a wizard kidnapped him and turned him into a tadpole. My poor little darling spent days in the swamp before we found him. His experience must have freed up the magic he inherited from me, because ever since then he's been able to turn into any kind of animal. He's a sweet boy and mostly chooses cuddly animals like kittens or puppies or lambs. He did turn into an enormous spider once, but even that was soft and fluffy and didn't bite. You can't imagine how startled I was when a huge spider jumped into my lap wanting to snuggle!"

Annie wasn't nearly as surprised as she might have been. She knew that magic was strong in Greater Greensward and that Millie's mother could turn into a dragon, so hearing that a little boy could turn into a puppy didn't seem so unlikely.

"You must be Millie's mother," said Annie. "I'm Princess Annabelle, although my friends call me Annie."

"Of course!" said the woman. "Millie and Audun told me all about you. They said that you're the one who told Millie that she was having a baby. My name is Princess Emeralda, but you may call me Emma. I'm delighted to meet you! I'm guessing that you're here to see Millie. She's upstairs in the tower. Audun is away right now, so Millie and I decided to see what clothes she's going to need for the baby. We were looking at Felix's old baby clothes when he ran off. Ah, I think I hear him again. Wait just a minute while I get him, then we'll take you up to Millie."

Annie sat down on the steps while Emma hurried behind the stable. When she came back she was carrying an adorable little boy with tousled red-gold curls and laughing blue eyes. Emma kissed him and the boy chortled as he laid his head against her chest.

"Felix, this is Annie, a friend of your sister Millie's," Emma told him.

"Hi!" the little boy said, squirming to get down.

"Not yet, little man," Emma said, and held him more tightly. "Not until we're upstairs again."

Annie followed them into the castle, smiling as Felix chattered about all the things he saw as a puppy. They climbed the winding stairs up the tower, stopping once so Emma could point out the sights through an arrow slit. When they reached the top, Emma opened the only door and ushered Annie inside.

"Millie, look who came to visit!" Emma exclaimed as she stepped aside so her daughter could see Annie standing behind her.

"Annie!" Millie shouted, and stood up from the window seat to greet her friend. "I didn't expect to see you!" She threw her arms around Annie, who hugged her back.

"Is everything all right?" Millie asked, looking into Annie's eyes. "I thought you were super busy getting ready for the coronation."

"We are, or we were at least, but then we got an urgent message from my parents," Annie told her. "People have been buying the Treecrest postcards at the Magic Marketplace, then going to my parents' castle in huge groups and holding parties in the great hall. This is all without my parents' permission, let alone invitation. I got rid of a rowdy group of witches, but I need help with another group. Millie, I think they're vampires, which is something we've never seen in our part of the world before. They took over the great hall last night, then this morning we found two unconscious guards with bite marks on their necks."

"And you came to see me because I told you that there are vampires here, didn't you?" said Millie. "I don't know how much help I can be, but Zoë might know what to do. She's half vampire and is married to my great-aunt Grassina's son, Francis."

"I believe Zoë and Francis are home today," said Emma. "Francis told me yesterday that he was planning to try out a new sword he bought at the Magic Marketplace."

"Then we should head over there," Millie announced. "I'll take you, Annie. I always like watching Francis practice anyway."

"And Felix and I will go visit the kitchen and see what treats Cook is baking today," said Emma. "Felix? Where did that boy go now? I shouldn't have set him down before." When she saw that the door to the adjoining room was standing open, she hurried in while calling her son's name.

Millie laughed. "From all the stories I've heard, I was a real handful when I was little, but I have a feeling that Felix is going to be even worse once he discovers everything he can do!"

"Do we need to help your mother find him?" Annie asked.

"We'd just get in the way," Millie told her. "If she really can't find him, Mother can use her magic and she'll know instantly where he's hiding. After that wizard took Felix, she cast a locater spell on him and can find him anywhere in the world now. Let me tell her that we're going and we can head out."

Annie waited while Millie went into the other room. Noticing a large, water-filled bowl on a table, she walked over to get a better look at the fish swimming inside. She gasped when she realized that they were sharks and that a tiny mermaid was chasing them off with a long horn that shot bubbles from the tip. Annie frowned and stepped closer. That mermaid looked awfully familiar.

"You've met Coral, haven't you?" Millie said, coming up behind her. "The bowl is a shortcut to her castle. She's a real terror with that magic narwhal horn. Let's go. Felix fell asleep on my bed and Mother is going to stay with him until he wakes up. He always gets tired when he's been a puppy. It's all that running around, I suppose."

"May I ask you a question about Felix?" Annie said as they started down the stairs. "You know that regular magic doesn't work around me. And I know that dragon magic does because it's the strongest magic there is, which is why you can still turn into a dragon when I'm near you. My question is—does Felix have dragon magic, too? Is that why he didn't turn back into a human when I touched him?"

"I'm sure it is," Millie said. "It's only a matter of time before he turns into a dragon. When he does, I have a feeling that we're really going to miss his kitten and puppy phase."

Annie looked around as they left the castle. The courtyard was bustling with everyday business, and the people all looked happy, as if they were exactly where they wanted to be. When she crossed the drawbridge and turned onto the road, she noticed the profusion of flowers planted along both sides.

"It smells wonderful here," Annie said, and took a deep breath.

"My mother started planting flowers after she broke a terrible family curse," Millie told her. "They couldn't have flowers anywhere near the castle before then. Just touching a flower would have turned a female member of the family over sixteen years old into a nasty hag. Mother refused to marry my father until after she broke the curse. Now she plants more flowers every year."

"This reminds me of the path to the meadow belonging to the fairy Sweetness N Light," said Annie. "Without the babbling brook and the pushy flower fairies. I like this much better. How far is it to Zoë's house?"

"Not far at all," said Millie. "It used to take a lot longer, but we go there so often that my grandfather had a road built to the river. We'll stay on this road for about half a mile, then turn left when we see the lightning-blasted tree. As my mother says, it's only a hop, skip, and a jump away. But that makes more sense if you're a frog. It's a short walk if you're a human."

The beautiful flowers, fresh air, and sunshine did a lot to lighten Annie's heart. When they reached the road that ran beside the river, she thought it was one of the prettiest places she'd ever seen. But when she saw a little cottage with a thatched roof and a woman tending her garden, she remembered why she had come to Greater Greensward. "Is that Zoë?" she asked her friend.

Millie laughed. "No, that's my mother's aunt, Grassina. She's Francis's mother. Zoë and Francis live just around the bend in the river."

Annie realized her mistake as they approached the cottage. While the woman bore a strong resemblance to both Emma and Millie, her hair was auburn shot with gray, and the laugh lines beside her mouth and eyes revealed her age. Rubbing her back as if it ached when she straightened up from weeding, she saw the girls and called, "Millie! What brings you out this way?"

"We're heading to Zoë's," Millie replied. "Do you know if she's home?"

"From the sounds I heard a minute ago, I'd say they're both home," said Grassina. "Are you going to introduce me to your friend?"

"Oh, I'm sorry!" Millie replied. "This is Annie. She's

from Treecrest, a kingdom on the other side of the world."

Grassina set her trowel on top of a sunflower; neither the trowel nor the flower budged as she extended her hand. "How nice to meet you," she said, taking Annie's hand in hers. The moment they touched, the sunflower bent over, dropping the trowel into the dirt.

"Annie is having a vampire problem and I thought Zoë might be able to help," Millie continued.

"A vampire problem? Oh, dear," Grassina replied. "I never liked vampires until I met Garrid. I love Zoë to pieces, but regular vampires are a different story. I wish you luck, Annie, and I hope Zoë is able to solve your problem."

"Thank you," Annie replied. "It was nice meeting you."

"And you," said Grassina. "Now, where did I put that trowel?"

"Sorry," said Annie. "That was my fault. Magic doesn't work around me."

"Oh, you're *that* friend! I remember Millie telling me about you," Grassina said. "It sounded as if you lead an interesting life."

"I think we all do, Aunt Grassina," Millie said with a laugh.

"That's true," Grassina replied. "So, if my magic isn't working now, my trowel should be right about…there." Glancing down, she spotted the trowel and picked it up. "So many weeds, so little time. I could use magic to do this, but I find gardening so relaxing. Blast! How did prickers get in my cucumbers?"

"She seems very nice," Annie said once she and Millie had started walking again.

"She's wonderful!" Millie told her. "She's also a powerful witch, although not nearly as powerful as my mother. But then, the Green Witch is the most powerful witch in the kingdom."

"And your mother is the Green Witch?" asked Annie.

Millie nodded. "She has regular magic *and* dragon magic. A witch can't get any more powerful than that. What on earth?" she said as a troll roared and stumbled onto the road ahead of them.

Annie froze, ready to run, but the troll didn't seem to notice the girls. Instead, he barreled down the road, heading straight for a lovely home set beside the river where a young man stood poised with a sword in his hand.

"Halt or face the consequences!" the young man shouted.

The troll roared so loudly that it hurt Annie's ears. With a mighty swing, the young man brought down his sword, whacking the troll on top of his head with the flat of the blade. The troll staggered, and fell to the ground, stunned. A moment later, he shimmered and disappeared.

"That was great, Torrin!" the young man cried. "I wasn't sure if you had enough strength to do that."

The sword began to sing:

I am a very powerful blade,
And I can do a lot.
I can cut through the thickest tree,
And slice off a—

"He'd better be strong considering how much you spent on him," said a girl sitting in the fork of a nearby tree. Her hair was such a pale blond that it looked almost white, and seemed to shine even in the shade. "I still don't know why you needed a singing sword." Swinging her legs over the side, she pushed off and landed on the ground.

"That troll wasn't real, was he?" Annie asked Millie.

Millie shook her head. "Francis is a wizard and a knight. He often combines the two and fights illusions as strong as the real thing for practice. Zoë and Francis, I'd like you to meet my friend Annie."

"You're the one that Millie told us about!" said Zoë. "Imagine, going through life without magic even touching you."

"It can be very useful at times," Annie told her.

"I bet!" said Francis.

"I brought Annie to meet you because she's having

a problem with vampires and I thought you might be able to help her," Millie said.

Annie nodded. "I understand you're part vampire, Zoë. How is that even possible?"

"My father is a vampire prince who can turn into a vampire bat. He was a bat when he fell in love with my mother, who's a regular brown bat. A lot of people were surprised when my parents got married, but they're very happy together. So, exactly what kind of problem are you having with vampires?"

"A group of them bought postcards from the Magic Marketplace and used them to visit my parents' kingdom, Treecrest," said Annie. "They held a dance in the great hall without my parents' permission, and bit two of our guards last night. Now we don't know how to get them to leave, or make sure they don't bite anyone else."

"First of all, someone must have invited them in, or they never could have made it through the door," Zoë told her.

"It was one of the witches," Annie replied. "They weren't invited, either, but they came in anyway. I was able to get rid of them, but it's the vampires that have me worried. They were led by a man, I mean a vampire, calling himself the Duke of Highcliff."

"Really? I know him and his friends. They can be forceful and intimidating. Francis, how would you like

56

to take a little trip with me? I think we should visit this...what did you call it? Treetop?"

"Treecrest," said Annie.

"If you think we should go there, my love, then we shall," said Francis. "Just let me change my clothes and I'll be ready in two shakes of a manticore's tail."

"I'll change, too. I seem to have gotten leaves in my hair and loose bits of bark on my gown," Zoë said, picking pieces off her skirt. "Will you be going with us, Millie?"

"Not today," Millie replied. "Audun won't be back from his trip until tonight and he'd be upset if I went on a trip like this without him. He's been very protective ever since we learned that we're expecting. I don't want to make him worry."

Annie felt a pang of guilt and looked away. Yes, she had left a note for Liam, but that wasn't the same as telling him in person. She had taken the postcard with her, too, so it wasn't as if he could follow her. The sooner she returned home, the better.

CHAPTER 6

IT WAS NIGHT when Annie and her companions arrived outside the castle in Treecrest. Annie was surprised that it was dark out until she remembered that she had traveled to the other side of the world and things were bound to be different.

Francis and Zoë looked around as they passed under the gates and entered the courtyard. "I thought everything would be exotic or unusual," Francis finally said, "but this looks like half the castles back home."

Annie was about to reply when she heard music coming from inside the castle. "The vampires are having another dance," she said, hurrying up the stairs.

"I've heard these musicians before," Zoë said. "They've played at some of my father's parties."

Annie was halfway down the corridor when she realized that Francis and Zoë weren't with her. She glanced back and saw them standing in the doorway. "What's wrong?" she asked.

"I can't come in without an invitation," said Zoë.

"And I'm not going anywhere without her," added Francis.

"Oh, right," Annie said. "In that case, please come in."

Although Zoë and Francis quickly caught up, acting as if nothing unusual had happened, the incident had reminded Annie that Zoë was in fact a vampire. For a second Annie wondered if she'd made the right choice in bringing Zoë there. "She's Millie's friend," she told herself. "And she's here to help."

The music grew louder as they approached the great hall and saw a cluster of guards standing just outside the door. Annie spotted Liam and Captain Sterling, and was hurrying over to talk to them when Squidge stepped in front of her.

"Ooh, are you in trouble now!" Squidge announced. "Liam was looking all over for you."

"I left a note!" Annie exclaimed. "Didn't he see it?"

Squidge looked away, no longer able to meet her eyes. "Yeah, about that. Someone might have been jumping on your bed with a cat and a hedgehog. And maybe the note fell on the floor. And maybe the hedgehog chewed it up. There are a couple of little pieces left, though. I can get them for you if you want."

"Squidge!" Annie cried.

The little sprite shrugged. "I was trying to get the lumps out of your bed so I could take a nap."

"Why didn't you tell Liam about the note?" asked Annie.

"Like I read it! Plus, he was so upset when I saw him that he wouldn't have listened to me even if I had tried to tell him," said Squidge. "Did you know that little veins stand out in his forehead when he's all worked up?"

"You said you had come to help us, but this was not helpful," Annie said through gritted teeth. "I'll talk to you later. Right now I have to talk to Liam."

"Fine, be like that," Squidge said, stepping out of her way. "No matter what I do, people always get mad at me!"

"Liam!" Annie called, hurrying to his side. "I'm so sorry I made you worry and I'm sorry I didn't wait for you, but there really wasn't time. Once I was sure I knew what those people are, I knew I had to hurry and find some help. I went to Greater Greensward to talk to Millie. I left you a note, but a hedgehog ate it."

"What?" he said, looking angry.

Annie shrugged. "Squidge and his friends were jumping on our bed. I'll tell you all about it later. I was hoping to be back before dark. Was anyone else bitten?"

"Not so far, although the night is still young," said Liam. "You don't know how worried I was. I had half the people in the castle looking everywhere for you. I understand why you went, but next time you're using a

60

postcard, please wait for me. There's no telling what can happen when those cards take you somewhere."

"I promise," Annie replied. "Although it would help if you'd let someone know where you're going so I can find you."

"You have a point," Liam said, and hugged her. "I'm just glad you're safe. You said you know something about those people?"

Annie nodded and turned to watch the dancers. This time they were wearing elaborate masks and matching outfits, making them look like bizarre birds and animals. Although the same musicians were play-ing, the music and dancing were wilder and faster.

"Millie had mentioned them, and I looked them up in one of Father's books," Annie told him. "They're vampires and can turn into bats. I went to Greater Greensward to find someone who can help us. Liam, Captain Sterling, this is Zoë and her husband, Francis." Annie turned to gesture to her companions. "Francis is the son of Millie's aunt. Zoë, Francis, I'd like you to meet my husband, Prince Liam, soon to be king of Dorinocco, and Captain Sterling, my parents' captain of the guard."

"It's an honor to meet you," said Francis.

"It is," said Zoë, "but if you'll excuse me, I want to see if I can find out what's going on. I'll tell you as soon as I know something."

"Zoë is half vampire," Annie told Liam as Zoë

61

walked away. "Her father is a vampire prince and she says she knows the Duke of Highcliff."

"Really?" said Liam. "Then maybe she can help. Do you think they'll listen to her if she tells them to go home?"

Annie shrugged. "I hope that's all it will take."

"If not, I'm sure she'll think of something," said Francis. "Her father has taught her a lot about dealing with vampires."

Zoë came back only a few minutes later. "I spoke with the Duke of Highcliff," she told Annie. "They bought those postcards with the intention of holding a week of festivities in a new place. He said they'll go somewhere else next year. When I told the duke that this wasn't fair to the owners of the castle, he argued that the vampires were invited in. I asked him to take his friends and go, but he refused. I bet he'd listen if my father were here."

"But they weren't invited in, at least not by the owners," said Annie. "This is my parents' castle. They didn't invite any of the postcard holders in. The witches let themselves in without an invitation, then one told the duke that he could come in, too."

"And then he invited his friends in," Zoë said, nodding. "I've heard of this happening before, but never on such a big scale."

"Did you say they intend to stay for a week?" asked Liam.

"Or longer," Zoë told him. "I know most of the vampires here. Sometimes their parties can get a little out of hand."

"Are those the guards who were bitten last night?" Annie asked, pointing at two of the dancers.

"They are," said Liam. "They woke as soon as it was dark and joined the vampires coming out of the cellar."

"They're vampires now," Zoë told them. "And there's no way to change them back."

"Isn't there anything we can do?" asked Annie. "We can't have the castle filled with vampires for an entire week!"

"Or more," Liam reminded her.

"Of course we can do something," said Zoë. "But I need to talk to your parents."

"They retired to His Majesty's chamber along with half the staff just before dark," Captain Sterling told Annie.

"I'll take you there," Annie told Zoë. "If we can end this, let's do it now."

Annie and Liam led Zoë and Francis up the stairs to King Halbert's chambers. Once again the footman was reluctant to let them in until they'd identified themselves. When he finally did open it, Annie and Liam walked in first. Seeing two strangers behind them, the footman almost slammed the door in Zoë's and Francis's faces, but Annie got in the way.

"Do you remember Audun and Millie and how

much they helped us when we were looking for a cure for you?" Annie asked her father. "These are their friends Zoë and Francis."

"Then they may enter," said the king, gesturing to the footman.

"Everyone is frightened," Queen Karolina told her daughter. "It's hard to trust strangers now."

"But Zoë and Francis are here to help," Annie replied. "Zoë knows what to do."

"You mean you know how to make them leave?" asked King Halbert.

"It's very simple," Zoë told the king and queen. "Most vampires are extremely self-centered and don't care about anyone else, but they do have a few rules that they have to follow. It's built into their very nature to obey these rules, although they do try to bend them when they can."

"And one of these rules can help us?" the queen asked.

Zoë nodded. "They pushed the limits on one of the most basic rules when the first vampire came in through another guest's invitation, and an uninvited guest at that. They aren't supposed to gain entry until a resident, preferably the owner, invites them in. All you have to do to get them to leave is to rescind the invitation. If it's the owner of the property, they'll leave that much faster."

"I'm ready," King Halbert declared, squaring his

shoulders. "I'll do whatever it takes to make them leave."

"Then go to the great hall and announce that they have to depart right now. Tell them that they are not welcome and cannot stay," said Zoë.

"That's it? That's all I have to do?" asked the king.

"That's it," said Zoë.

"Then what happens?" Liam asked.

"You'll see," Zoë replied, and led the way out the door.

All the guards who had been stationed in the king's chamber to protect him accompanied the royal family down the stairs. As they walked, more guards joined them until the king had a sizable group around him when he finally reached the great hall. Even Squidge joined their ranks, looking stern and determined.

The musicians were playing a frenzied waltz when the king stepped inside the room. None of the vampires seemed to notice that he was there. Francis was standing a good distance from Annie when he declared in a magically amplified voice, "Attention everyone! The king of Treecrest has an announcement to make."

The music trailed off to a final fading tootle on the flute, the dancers stopped spinning across the room, and every vampire turned to face King Halbert. The king cleared his throat, held his head high, and said, "I am King Halbert, ruler of this kingdom and owner of this castle. Vampires are not welcome here. You must all leave now and never come back. Your unauthorized invitation has been rescinded. Now, get out!"

Annie heard the whistling of the wind before she felt it. Suddenly, it was whipping around the great hall, swirling the long, flowing dresses of the female vampires and blowing the musicians' instruments from their hands. A moment later it was dragging the vampires out of the hall and down the corridor, even as it pushed the humans back.

"No!" screamed the vampires, unable to fight the wind.

"That looks like fun!" shouted Squidge. Running into the hall, he grabbed hold of a vampire's leg and held on.

The door to the courtyard opened with a bang and the vampires shot out the door one after the other.

Annie was relieved to see them go and didn't realize that anything was wrong until she heard Francis shout, "Zoë!"

Turning her head, she saw the slender young woman dragged across the floor just like the rest of the vampires. And then Zoë was out the door while her husband strained against the force of that very same wind, trying to follow her.

CHAPTER 7

"Zoë!" Francis cried again, struggling against the wind that held him back.

"I wonder if she knew that was going to happen," Liam said to Annie.

"She didn't look surprised, so I think she had a good idea that it would," said Annie. "Yet she did it anyway. I like that girl!"

Suddenly there was another loud bang and the wind stopped. Francis staggered. When he caught his balance, he started to run toward the door.

"Stop him!" Liam shouted, and three of the guards jumped to restrain Francis.

"I have to go!" Francis exclaimed, trying to pull away.

"You can't run after your wife like that," said Liam. "The vampires are gone, but we don't know where they went. It's dark out and they could be anywhere, including right outside the door."

"But Zoë is out there, too!" said Francis.

"And she's a vampire. Do you really think they'd hurt one of their own?" Liam asked.

"But she isn't, at least not to the more traditionally minded vampires," Francis told him. "Her mother isn't a vampire, so some vampires don't hold Zoë in the same regard as they do her father. You should hear some of the nasty things they say about her. Even the ones who accept her might be angry. I'm sure they've figured out that she was the one who told King Halbert how to evict them. Vampires don't like being thwarted, especially when they're enjoying themselves. They'll be mad now and will want to come in again. If certain vampires find her, they could threaten to hurt Zoë if we don't let them come back in the castle. Don't you see? I have to save her and bring her back."

"Then I'm going with you," said Liam. "But first we need to get ready. Going out there to face all those vampires unprepared could be deadly."

"I'm ready now," Francis declared.

"But I'm not," said Liam. "We'll both need suits of armor so they can't bite us, and weapons to fend them off. We need torches to light our way and more people to help us or we won't stand a chance against so many."

"I'm going with you!" Annie declared. "I can wear the suit of armor that Snow White gave me. I never took it to Dorinocco."

"Annie, you can't mean it!" her mother exclaimed. "It's much too dangerous."

"Zoë came to help us," Annie told her. "She knew that the wind would carry her out with the others and that was dangerous, too. Now it's my turn to help her."

"I'll go as well," Captain Sterling declared.

"As will I!" shouted the knights.

Soon Annie, Liam, and all the knights in the castle had run off to collect their armor and weapons, leaving Francis behind with the king and queen. Annie got a maid to help strap her into the small suit of armor that almost but didn't quite fit. When she returned downstairs, her mother took one look at her and shook her head. "I really don't approve of this. You're about to become queen of a kingdom and here you are going out to fight vampires. How do you know that armor will even keep you safe?"

"I wore this armor when birds were attacking me," said Annie. "I'm sure it will do just as well against bats. And no vampires will be able to bite my neck as long as I'm wearing this. Francis, look at you! I've never seen armor made of gold before. Isn't gold too soft to protect you?"

"Not this gold," said Francis. "I've used magic to enhance it. Just don't come near me when we're out there, Annie. I don't want the magic to fade."

"He conjured it out of nowhere," said Queen Karolina. "I didn't know he was a wizard."

69

"And warrior," Francis told her. "I've been studying magic and the fighting arts my whole life. Here, I can do something about lighting our way, too. Where I come from, these are called witches' lights." With a few words and gestures, Francis created one glowing ball after another. Some were the size of cantaloupes while others were bigger than watermelons, but they all gave off the same warm glow. As Liam and the knights returned to the room, he attached an invisible tether to each suit of armor. "Sorry, Annie," he said when he was done. "There's no use giving you one. It wouldn't work around you."

"That's all right," said Liam. "I'll keep Annie close to me."

"Before we go, everyone who is staying behind should know that the vampires will probably try to come back in," Francis announced. "They'll beg, wheedle, and threaten, saying whatever they think will get them invited inside. Ignore everything they say. Look the other way if you see one in a window or doorway. They can be very convincing when they want to be."

"Spread the word throughout the castle," Liam said to the people gathered around. "Everyone needs to know this or we're all in trouble."

"Everyone who is going with me—be as quiet as you can," said Francis. "Vampires are attracted to loud noises."

"I'll do my best, but there's no way I can be

70

completely quiet when I'm wearing armor," Annie whispered to Liam. "When I walk, I sound like someone is banging pots and pans together."

Liam grunted and said, "We all do. This should be loads of fun."

Francis started out the door first, his golden armor shining like a beacon for everyone to follow. Liam kept glancing at the witches' light trailing a few feet behind him as he walked, but when it didn't get tangled or stuck on anything, he seemed to forget that it was there. Annie walked beside Liam, trying not to clank in the armor that pinched here and squeezed there. It had been made for a boy and fit like it. She wondered if she should get some armor made for her in case she was going to keep needing it.

Annie's helmet made it hard to see much, but when Francis opened the door from the corridor to the courtyard outside, she peered around him, trying to see if any vampires were lurking on the steps. As far as she could see, there wasn't anyone there.

"Take my arm," Liam told her as they approached the door. "It's hard to go down stairs when you can't see where you're going."

"It doesn't seem to bother you," Annie said, holding on to him.

"I'm used to it," he replied. "I got my first suit of armor when I was six years old."

It was a moonless night, and with much of the

71

courtyard dark, the only light came from torches mounted at intervals on the castle walls and on either side of the gatehouse. As the search party descended the steps, their witches' lights followed them, creating moving pools of light. Liam's light had gone out as soon as Annie took his hand, but the lights tethered to the other knights still made it easy to see.

When they reached Francis, he was standing in the middle of the courtyard, looking around. "I'm sure Zoë is here somewhere," he said. "She wouldn't have gone far because she'd know that I'd come after her. I'm going to look by the dovecote, if that's what that is. It looks like a giant beehive."

"It was a dovecote until yesterday. I forgot that one of the visiting witches changed it. I'll have to see about turning it back tomorrow," Annie told him.

While Francis made his way to the former dovecote, Annie turned to Liam. "I think Zoë will have gone somewhere sheltered, but not inside any buildings where she'd have to get an invitation. Let's look in my mother's garden. There are lots of places to hide there."

"Do you think she's hiding?" asked Liam.

"Wouldn't you be if you had made vampires angry?" Annie asked him.

"Zoë's never been here before. She wouldn't know that the garden was behind that wall," said Liam.

"Of course she'd know!" Annie said, her voice loud inside the helmet. "You can smell the flowers as soon as you walk out the door. And lots of walled gardens have hidden niches and tall shrubs that are perfect for hiding. If you don't want to look there, I can go by myself. That garden is where I'd hide if I were Zoë."

"I'm coming," said Liam. "I can't have you wandering around in the dark by yourself."

"Good!" Annie declared. "I'd much rather wander around with you. Have you seen Squidge? The wind carried him outside, too."

"I saw him grab hold of a vampire. Squidge wanted to go."

"Did someone say my name?" Squidge asked from out of the dark.

Annie had to stop and lean over, turning her head inside her helmet until she could see him. "You shouldn't pop up like that," she told him. "I can barely see what's in front of me and I could have stepped on you."

"I saw you walking around all stiff like a toy made out of sticks," Squidge told her. "I haven't laughed that hard in hours. Why are you wearing a metal skin?"

"It's a suit of armor," said Annie. "We're wearing them so the vampires can't bite us."

"Oh, right! That's what I wanted to tell you. I followed the vampires to see what they'd do. A lot of them turned into bats and flew off when they got out here, but some of them are lurking in the shadows. I'll go look for some so you can poke them with your swords.

Ready or not, vampires, here I come!" the little sprite shouted.

"Now that was definitely not quiet," Liam muttered as the sprite ran off into the dark.

Squidge had scarcely disappeared when a sound like rushing water came from the gatehouse and bats poured into the courtyard. Annie and Liam moved closer to each other and stood back-to-back with their swords raised. The bats swooped down on the search party, attempting to reach them while avoiding the slashing swords. Annie and Liam shuffled closer to the garden even as they tried to fend off the bats. After a half dozen bats had fallen to the ground, motionless, the others retreated.

While the knights readied themselves for the next onslaught, Annie and Liam took advantage of the lull to run across the courtyard. They had just opened the gate when the bats fell on the searchers again. Curiously, none of the bats followed Annie and Liam into the garden.

"Now what?" Liam asked Annie.

"Now we look for a place where she might hide," Annie told him. "Wait, is that Francis?"

The young knight was standing on the garden path, holding something in his hand. When Annie drew close enough to see, she realized that it was a black dragon's scale that flashed blue if he turned it one way and red if he turned it another. "What are you doing?" she asked.

"Looking for Zoë," said Francis. "I remembered that I had this in my storage acorn. My mother gave it to me. It goes red if I'm heading in the right direction and blue if I'm not. There, it's red again. She's over this way."

"In the rosebushes?" Annie asked, surprised as they headed that way.

"That's what it says," Francis declared as he hurried down the path. "Zoë, are you there? It's me, Francis."

"You came for me!" a little bat cried, creeping out of the shrub. With a flutter of wings, the bat landed in front of Francis. A moment later, Zoë the girl was there, throwing her arms around her husband despite his suit of armor.

"Did you really doubt that I would look for you?" he murmured into her hair.

"Uh, guys, we have company," Liam said as bats surrounded them, only to resume their human forms.

Annie's helmet kept her from seeing anything that wasn't directly in front of her, but she heard a vampire say, "We were waiting for you to find her for us. You're not leaving here with that half-breed princess."

"And you're not getting anywhere near her," Francis announced. "Zoë, stay behind me. Annie, don't get too close. I need my magic to work."

Liam put his arm around Annie and they both

stepped away, turning to face the approaching vampires.

"Lumen!" Francis shouted, and a bright pulse of light shot from his suit of armor. The vampires cried out, covering their eyes with their arms and capes and falling back a few paces. A moment later, the pounding of feet and rattling of armor announced the arrival of Captain Sterling and his knights.

Even as the vampires rushed at him with swords drawn, Francis cried, "Awake, Torrin!" and drew his own sword from its scabbard. With a mighty stroke, he hacked at the advancing vampires, driving them back as his sword began to sing:

> *Away from us, you nasty foe*
> *Dare not to draw so near*
> *I'd gladly slice your nose right off,*
> *Leave you with half an ear.*
> *And if you come at us again,*
> *Just know I'll do my part*
> *I'll turn a little lower then,*
> *And aim straight for your heart.*

While Francis and Torrin were able to force the vampires to retreat, Liam was just as valiant. Annie used her sword to protect his back as he followed Francis and Zoë across the garden, slashing and hacking at their assailants. Captain Sterling and his knights spread out around the garden, taking on the vampires lurking behind their friends. The fighting was fierce until one by one, the vampires turned into bats and flew off. Finally, only Zoë and the humans were left behind.

"Wow!" Squidge said, peeking into the garden. "That was really something! I didn't know that you guys could fight like that."

"What is that creature?" Francis asked. "I've never seen his kind before."

"He's a sprite," said Liam. "He may look innocent enough, but he can make more trouble than a room full of vampires."

"I like that!" said Squidge. "Do you mind if I quote you?"

"Do whatever you want," Liam replied. "You always do."

CHAPTER 8

BEFORE THE VAMPIRES REGROUPED, Francis and Zoë ran to the castle door hand in hand, with Annie and Liam only a few paces behind them.

"Quick!" Francis shouted at Annie. "Invite Zoë in."

"Zoë, please come in!" Annie hurried to say, then they all ran in at once while Captain Sterling and his knights brought up the rear. As soon as the door was shut and bolted, Annie took off her helmet and sighed with relief.

"No one should go outside for the rest of the night unless they're wearing a suit of armor," Liam announced.

Annie nodded in agreement. "If we're lucky, the vampires will go home tonight and we'll never see them again. I hope this is the last group of uninvited guests. I don't know if my mother's nerves could take any more."

Zoë gave Francis an odd look, but neither one said anything.

Conway, the castle steward, hurried up with a group of worried servants behind him. "Everyone is wondering if we'll be safe now," the steward said, glancing from Annie to Liam.

"You should be, provided you stay inside until dawn," said Liam.

"Do you have a room we could use tonight?" Francis asked. "Zoë is exhausted." His wife was leaning against him, yawning so broadly that Annie could see her pointed vampire teeth.

"Of course!" Annie exclaimed. "I should have offered sooner. I'm sure Conway can find you one. Thank you so much for helping us. I don't know what we would have done without you."

"We're glad we could help," Francis replied.

As the steward escorted Zoë and Francis down the corridor, Annie turned to Liam. "I'm going upstairs to get out of this suit of armor."

"I'll be along as soon as I've talked to Captain Sterling," Liam told her. "I think we should stand guard inside the castle just in case."

"Good night, everyone," Annie said, and started for her room.

Tired from wearing the armor and with its weight still slowing her down, she took longer than usual to climb the stairs. She was trudging down the corridor when she saw a maid and asked her to come along to help her unfasten the armored pieces. Hot and sweaty from wearing the armor, Annie sent a footman for bath water.

The water was a little hot at first, but as Annie got used to it, she sank down and relaxed. Her eyes were half closed and she was nearly asleep when she heard something scraping on the window. Thinking it was an owl or a confused bird, she turned her head and opened her eyes. A shape moved on the other side of the glass. Annie gasped when she realized that it was a face. One of the vampires was right outside her window

"Let me in!" cried the vampire, moving closer until he was almost touching the glass. "We need to talk."

"Are you flying?" Annie asked. "This is the third floor. How can you be up here?" She started to get out for a better look, but hurriedly sat down again when the cool air touched her wet skin and she remembered where she was.

"Just let me in and I'll tell you everything you want to know," the vampire said in a cajoling voice.

Annie frowned. "How long have you been out there?" she asked.

"Long enough," he said, leering.

Annie's face turned red and she sank deeper into the water. "Go away!" she shouted.

"But I have so much to tell you," replied the vampire.

The door opened and Liam stepped in. "Sorry it took me so long," he said, then noticed where Annie was looking. "There's a vampire here, too? Your parents had the same problem. The vampires wouldn't leave until we covered the windows with tapestries." He looked around the room and shook his head. "There aren't enough tapestries in here to cover all the windows, so I'll have to send for more and get some footmen to help me put them up."

"Can you use something else for now so I can get out of the tub?" Annie cried. "This is so embarrassing."

"I suppose I can use a blanket," Liam said, looking around. "But the tapestries—"

There was a knock on the door and it burst open, admitting Squidge, who was once again riding on Dash's back.

"Did someone call my name?" the sprite asked as he rode into the room, waving a long knife in the air.

"No!" Annie and Liam both said.

"Well, you should have," said Squidge. "I can take care of this for you."

"What is that?" asked the vampire.

"It looks like a kitchen knife to me," said Liam.

The vampire shook his head. "I meant the little delicious-looking creature."

"I'm your worst nightmare," Squidge told him.

"Squidge, you need to leave!" said Annie. "And Liam, would you please put that blanket over the window? I really don't like company when I'm in the bathtub."

The sprite kicked Dash, making the hound leap forward. When Squidge was close enough, he climbed onto the windowsill. "I'm here so you can bite me!" Squidge shouted at the vampire as he pulled down his collar. "See my neck! Don't you wanna bite it? But you can't get it because you're out there and I'm in here."

"You're not helping, Squidge," said Annie.

Squidge held his collar down and wiggled his body, chanting, "Nanny nanny, boo boo. You can't get me!"

"I don't have to listen to this!" the vampire cried. There was a flurry of movement outside the window and he was gone.

"I can't believe I'm saying this, but thanks for coming in, Squidge," Annie said. "Now, would you mind leaving the room so I can finish my bath? This water is getting cold."

Squidge hopped onto Dash's back and turned the hound toward the door. "That's something I don't understand about humans. Why take a bath when you smell nice and ripe without one? My mother always told me that baths remove your natural body oils and are bad for you. I remember when—"

"Good-bye, Squidge," Liam said, shooing Dash out the door and shutting it behind him.

"Would you please put the tapestries over the windows?" Annie asked her husband. "I won't get any sleep if I think that vampire might come back. But let me get in my nightgown first. I'd prefer to have clothes on before anyone else comes in the room."

Even with tapestries over all the windows, Annie didn't sleep very well that night. The vampires were still outside the castle, calling to the people inside. Sticking her fingers in her ears and placing a pillow over her head didn't fully block out the sound of their voices and they haunted her dreams the few times she did manage to fall asleep. The vampires didn't stop calling until the first rays of the sun touched the tallest of the castle turrets and the roosters began to crow. Annie fell into a deeper sleep then, determined that she'd do something about the vampires that very day.

꙰

Annie and Liam slept late that morning, but they weren't the only ones. When they went downstairs to the great hall, they found Zoë, Francis, and Annie's parents seated on the dais, eating their breakfast, while Captain Sterling and a group of tired-looking knights sat a few tables away. Annie had scarcely taken her seat on the dais before she turned to Zoë and Francis. "Did you have any idea that the vampires might stay around?"

Zoë shrugged. "I was afraid they would, but I really hoped they'd go. I didn't want to worry you unnecessarily."

"Next time you're not sure if you should tell me

something, please don't hesitate. I'd rather worry and be prepared than be completely taken by surprise," Annie said, stifling a yawn.

There was a flurry of activity by the door to the hall and two guards hurried in. They spoke to Captain Sterling, who stood and approached the king's table. "Three people in the village were bitten last night," he told King Halbert. "Two men and a woman are lying unconscious in their beds."

"Send men to the village to warn everyone that they must stay inside after dark and not open their doors for anyone, no matter who they say they are or what they want," the king told the captain.

"What about the people who were already bitten?" asked Liam. "They can't stay with their families if they're going to turn into vampires."

"Will they definitely turn?" Annie asked Zoë.

"Probably," Zoë told her. "Although nothing is ever certain."

"Then they should be isolated," said Liam. "At least until we know one way or another."

"Liam, I don't know what we would have done if you and Annie hadn't come to help," Queen Karolina told him. "This whole thing terrifies me. Halbert and I have never had to deal with anything like this before."

"Is there anything we can do to make the vampires leave the kingdom?" Annie asked Zoë and Francis.

"I don't know of anything," said Francis.

"Neither do I," Zoë told her. "Most of them were very respectful, but they stopped listening when I told them they had to leave. They were having too much fun, and that's one thing vampires hate to give up. The only one they might listen to is my father. He has authority over all the vampires. Although he's usually very sweet, he's the most powerful vampire in our part of the world and knows how to make them obey him. I've asked him to teach me how he does it, but we haven't gotten to it yet."

"Could we ask him to help us?" the king asked Zoë.

"We could," Zoë replied. "Except there's one problem. My parents are on their annual tour of the vampire lands. I don't know where they'd be right now or how to get hold of them."

"Then I guess we need to go find them," said Annie. "I don't think we have any time to waste."

"It may take me a while," Zoë told her. "Especially if my father is busy with negotiations. The vampires he's visiting can be difficult to deal with."

"I'll go with you so I can convince him to come straight here. I can be very convincing when I try," Annie said.

Liam laughed. "You aren't kidding," he said.

CHAPTER 9

"WHAT DO YOU MEAN you want me to stay here?" Liam asked after Annie told him her plans a few hours later. "You know that I don't want you traveling by postcard alone."

"I won't be alone," said Annie. "I'm going with Zoë and Francis. I know you want to go, and I would be much happier if you did, but my mother asked if you could stay here. She's terrified of the vampires and says that she feels much safer with you protecting the castle. Captain Sterling said that it was your idea to put the tapestries over the windows, which helped a lot. Plus, you're the best non-magical swordsman he's ever seen. Please stay in Treecrest, Liam. I won't worry about my parents so much if you're looking out for them."

"I'll watch out for Annie," said Francis. "Zoë and I both will."

"I'll be fine," Annie assured her husband.

"So will Liam," Squidge told her. "Dash, Scarface, and Bumpo will help me take care of him."

"Who are Scarface and Bumpo?" Annie asked.

"You know—the cat and the hedgehog," said Squidge.

"Good luck with that," Annie murmured to her husband. When he looked as if he was going to object again, she kissed him until he forgot what he was going to say.

Zoë and Francis were standing on either side of Annie with their hands on her shoulders when she added, "Just be sure that everyone stays inside after dark." Liam opened his mouth, but Annie touched the center of the postcard she was holding before he could speak...and they were gone.

ॐ

The sun was setting when they arrived in front of the castle in Greater Greensward. The guards stationed on either side of the drawbridge nodded when they saw the new arrivals, but neither of them seemed surprised.

"Where should we go first?" Annie said, turning to Francis and Zoë.

"Probably inside the castle," Zoë said. "We can ask if anyone has seen either of my parents lately. Emma and my mother are best friends, so my mother would have come straight here as soon as they got back."

Francis and Zoë held hands as they started across the drawbridge. Annie turned to say something to Liam, then remembered that he wasn't there. She felt odd, as if a vital part of her were missing. Although it had been her choice not to have Liam come along, and she had only just left him, she began to wonder if she'd made the right decision. He had been an important part of her life since the night he found her in the forest while she was searching for a prince to kiss her sister. Leaving him in Treecrest to protect her parents had seemed like a good idea, but actually going somewhere without him was a lot harder than she'd expected.

Annie tried not to think about Liam as she followed her two new friends up the steps and into the castle. "You act as if this is your home," she said to Zoë. "Shouldn't we tell someone that we're here?"

"This is our home in a way," Francis told her as they headed for the great hall. "My mother is Queen Chartreuse's sister and Princess Emma's aunt. My grandparents are ghosts in the dungeon. I spent as much time here as in my parents' house when I was growing up."

"And Millie and I have been best friends our whole lives," said Zoë. "My brothers and I often stayed here when my parents couldn't take us with them when they traveled. My father has a castle in the mountains, but we like it better here, where it isn't so cold and isolated. Vampire castles tend to be gloomy, too. I can't take gloomy for more than a few days."

"How long is your father usually gone on his tours?" Annie asked as they entered the great hall.

Zoë shrugged. "That depends on who he's going to see and what he runs across. Sometimes it's only a few weeks, and sometimes it's a few months. Things always take longer when you can't work during daylight hours."

"Why are *you* able to go out in daylight?" Annie asked her.

"Because I'm only half vampire. My father always says that I lucked out. Two of my younger brothers can't go out in daylight, but they're both uncivilized and no one wants them out then anyway. Excuse me. There's the steward. He should be able to tell me where I can find Emma and Millie."

Zoë walked up to the man who had just entered the hall. When she came back, she said, "Emma is in the stable with her husband, Eadric, and Millie is upstairs taking a nap, or at least that's what she does every day before supper. I think we should go see Emma first."

They found Emma in a stall with a man who was brushing a white stallion. A plaque on the stall read *Bright Country*.

"Emma!" Francis said when he spotted her. "We need your help."

Emma looked up and smiled. "You're back! Did you get rid of the vampires?"

89

Annie stepped into the doorway so Emma could see her.

"Yes and no," she told Emma.

"Hi, Annie," said Emma. "Eadric, this is the girl I told you about who lives on the other side of the world. Princess Annabelle, I'd like you to meet my husband, Prince Eadric."

"Hi!" Eadric said, turning away from the horse long enough to smile at Annie. The horse nickered and bumped him with his head, making Eadric laugh and start brushing him again. "Sorry I stopped! Don't worry, I'm not finished yet."

"Zoë and Francis were a big help in getting the vampires out of the castle, but we don't know how to make them leave the kingdom," Annie told Emma. "They refuse to leave and are plaguing the people of Treecrest."

"I don't know what to do about it," said Zoë. "We were hoping my father could help. Do you know if he's back yet?"

Emma shook her head. "We haven't seen him in weeks, but Audun might be able to help you. He should return from visiting the ice dragon king soon. I understand he was going to make a few stops on the way back. It's possible that he's heard something."

The horse whinnied and stomped his hoof.

"All right, I'll tell her," Eadric said to the horse.

Turning toward Annie, he pointed at the stallion. "Brighty says that he heard Audun land in the courtyard a little while ago. He's probably with Millie now."

When Annie gave him a confused look, Zoë explained, "Emma and Eadric can talk to animals. We all can because we've been animals at one time or another."

"Eadric and I were frogs when we met," said Emma.

"Zoë is a bat half the time, and she's convinced me to turn into one on occasion," Francis added. "It makes me look at everything in a whole new way."

"Okay," Annie said, marveling that anyone could take such magical things so lightly.

"Let me see if Millie is awake," Emma told them. "She hasn't been feeling well and usually takes a nap right about now." Tugging on the chain around her neck, she showed them the crystal ball hanging on the end. "I can see a lot in my far-seeing ball and ... yes, Millie's awake and talking to Audun. You can go see her."

Annie gasped when she saw the image of Millie and Audun sitting on the window seat. She'd never seen magic like this before.

"Then we'll head up to the tower," Zoë said. "Thanks for your help."

"You're welcome," said Emma. "Although we really didn't do anything."

When the horse nickered, Eadric laughed and said, "You're right, Brighty. You were a help when you told them that Audun was back."

⁂

They were walking through the castle when Annie told Zoë, "I'm not used to all this magic working around me. First Felix stayed a puppy when I touched him, and now your mother made her magic far-seeing ball work, even though I was standing beside her. Back home, no one's magic does what they want when I'm around."

"Years ago, when Emma became a 'Dragon Friend,' her magic became extra powerful. It grew even stronger when she was finally able to turn herself into a dragon. She passed that strength on to her children, and nothing is stronger than dragon magic," said Zoë. "Not even a vampire's."

"What can vampires do besides turn into bats?" Annie asked her.

"Put people into trances, fly without wings, move without making a sound, light candles…nothing good, really."

"Would their magic trances work on me?" asked Annie.

"I don't know and I hope we never find out," Zoë replied.

Millie and Audun were still sitting side by side,

holding hands, when Annie and her friends walked in. Millie looked tiny next to her handsome husband, whose white hair drew everyone's eyes. The young couple looked delighted to see Annie. "You're back!" Millie cried.

"Hi, Annie," said Audun. "It's good to see you again. Isn't Liam with you?"

Annie shook her head. "He stayed in Treecrest to help my parents. They're terrified of vampires and don't really know what to do."

"What vampires?" Audun asked. "I don't remember seeing any when I was in Treecrest."

"People have been using magic postcards to go to Treecrest," said Annie. "I was able to get rid of the witches who came, but I needed Zoë's help to get the vampires out of the castle. They won't leave the kingdom, though."

"And they've been turning people into vampires without permission," Zoë added. "Father will be so mad! I'm afraid I've made a mess of things, though. I told Annie's father how to make the vampires leave the castle, and now they're furious with me. You know how much some of the nobles don't like me."

"Only a few!" said Francis. "And most of them still respect you."

Zoë shrugged. "All I know is that they wouldn't have acted the way they did if my father had been there. We really need his help now, so we came here hoping that he was back. Emma told us that he isn't and suggested that we talk to you. Did you hear anything about him during your travels?" she asked Audun.

"Not a thing," he said. "But then, I didn't stop anywhere that vampires usually visit. Do you know where he was headed?"

"I've gone with my parents enough to know the route they usually take. The problem is, he could be anywhere along the route by now."

"We'll have to go look for him," said Annie. "We can start where he usually goes first, then move on from there. Is his first stop very far from here?"

"It is," Zoë told her. It's in Upper Montevista in a village called Tottington."

"I wish I could take you, but I'm not turning into a dragon again until after the baby is born," Millie told them. "Audun, I know you just got back..."

"I'd be happy to help!" he said, getting to his feet. "As long as you're sure that you don't need me, my love."

"I'll be fine," Millie said with a laugh. "My parents will see to that. Good luck, Annie. I hope you find Garrid soon."

⁊

Remembering how cold it was to ride an ice dragon, Annie borrowed warm clothes from Millie while Francis and Zoë hurried home to get ready. They met in the castle courtyard a short time later. When Audun turned into a pale-blue-and-white dragon, Annie gave him a dubious look. "Are you sure you can carry all three of us?" she asked.

"Oh, I won't go like this," Zoë said, and a moment later had turned into a bat. She fluttered to Francis, who opened his coat, revealing a pouch sewn into the inside just above his heart. Zoë the bat slipped into the pouch so that only her head was showing.

"She'll stay nice and warm with me," Francis declared, closing his coat and gently patting his chest.

"That solves that," Annie said as she climbed onto Audun's back. As soon as Francis climbed on behind her, Audun took off, circling the tower once. They all waved at Millie and Emma, who were watching from the window.

"Upper Montevista, here we come!" Audun announced, and turned to head north.

They flew for the rest of the day, stopping occasionally to stretch their legs and eat. Annie and Francis ate some of the food that Zoë had packed while the little bat flew off to catch bugs, returning each time just as Annie and Francis finished eating. "I'll eat when we stop for the night," Audun told them. "I don't like to fly on a full stomach."

With the powerful wings of a dragon carrying them, they reached Tottington soon after the moon came out. Looking down from above, Annie noticed that the village wasn't like any she had ever seen before.

A single ring of houses surrounded an empty field, forming an oval. The houses were spaced so closely together that they looked like one continuous building from a distance, but as they drew closer, she could see that narrow spaces separated them.

Annie looked around as they landed, wondering at the houses' steeply pitched roofs and curious lack of windows on the lower floors. Candles lit the windows of the upper floors, making the houses look oddly unbalanced. Although she saw shadows moving inside the houses, no one came out to greet them or ask why they were there.

"They're afraid of me," Audun said as Francis helped Annie to the ground. "Give them a few minutes."

After folding his wings against his body, Audun turned back into a young man. He was standing beside Annie as a human when the first man came out of a house.

"Who are you, stranger? What do you want?" the man asked as he approached.

It was dark in the clearing with only the light of the half-moon to see by, but even so Annie could tell he was a vampire. Part of it was that his scent reminded her of the way the vampires had smelled when they came out of the cellar at home. Part of it was the way he moved, seeming to glide rather than walk.

Annie stepped closer to Audun when other doors

opened and more vampires emerged. She glanced at Francis when he opened his coat and Zoë fluttered to the ground. The vampires walked without making a sound; not one of them spoke again, or coughed or made any of the little noises that a large group of people always make. It was unnatural and it made Annie shiver and pull the collar of her coat more tightly closed.

"Corbin!" Zoë called, stepping away from her friends. "It's me, Princess Zoë."

"Princess!" the vampire who seemed to be the leader said, his excitement obvious in his voice. "We weren't expecting you. What a pleasant surprise!"

As word spread that their princess was there, the mood suddenly changed. The tenseness that had seemed to pervade the clearing was gone, and Annie felt her body relax. She told herself that she shouldn't have been afraid, considering who was with her. After all, Zoë was a vampire and knew these people, Francis was a warrior magician, and Audun was an actual dragon. Even so, there was some primal thing about vampires that made good sense go out the window and let terror in.

Annie, Francis, and Audun stepped out of the way as the vampires gathered around Zoë, pushing her friends aside, although none of them dared get close to Audun. The vampires were grinning now, and Zoë was talking and laughing with them. After a few minutes, Annie

97

exchanged glances with Francis. He shrugged and raised one eyebrow, then turned to his wife and called, "Zoë, we came to ask a question."

"Oh, right!" Zoë exclaimed. She pushed through the crowd, smiling and nodding until she reached her husband's side. Taking his hand in hers, she turned back to the vampires. "This is my husband, Prince Francis, as I'm sure you recall. And these are my friends Princess Annabelle and Audun. We came here hoping that you could help us. Has my father been here to see you lately?"

Anne noticed the looks the vampires gave each of them. They seemed disdainful when they studied her and Francis, but she thought she saw fear in their eyes when they glanced at Audun.

"Your father was here just last week," said Corbin. "Why don't we go in my house, where we can talk?" Bowing low, he waved his hand, gesturing at one of the houses.

When Zoë, Corbin, and Francis led the way, Annie hurried to keep up. She tried not to glance back at the vampires walking behind them, just as silent as they had been before. Audun didn't seem at all nervous, but she noticed that the vampires continued to keep their distance from him. She was relieved when Corbin opened his front door and they could step inside, shutting the rest of the vampires out.

Annie crinkled her nose when she took her next

breath. Looking around, she saw that they were in a large room with a table and chairs for six people. Although the house looked clean, the air smelled dank and earthy, like freshly overturned soil. She stood by the door, not sure what to do until Zoë gestured to her.

"Please, sit!" Corbin said, pulling a chair from the table for Zoë. "Suli! Drinks for our guests!"

A moment later, a vampire woman hurried through an inner door carrying a pitcher. Another woman who looked just like her followed with a tray of mugs and a plate of small cakes. After setting the pitcher and the tray on the table, they stood back, smiling at Zoë. Annie noticed that all three of their hosts had piercing eyes like the vampires who had invaded Treecrest.

"Please pardon my wife and her sister," said Corbin. "It isn't often that we have our princess at our table. Suli, Sharla, you may leave us now."

The two vampire women seemed reluctant to walk away. When they closed the door behind them, Annie had a feeling that they were still on the other side, listening.

After all his guests were seated with drinks and cakes in front of them, Corbin looked at Zoë expectantly. "You were asking about your father," he prompted.

Zoë nodded. "Yes. We're trying to find him, so we're retracing his itinerary. Was he here long?"

Corbin shook his head. "Just a few hours, as he normally is. We always appreciate his visits, but we do wish that he and your mother could stay longer. We were the first vampire community to learn that they were getting married, you know. We've felt a special connection to your family ever since."

"I know," said Zoë. "We feel it, too. Do you know if he was headed to Heartsblood Manor after this?"

"He did mention that," Corbin told her. "He stays the night there, doesn't he? I know it isn't fancy, but we do have rooms upstairs that could accommodate him, should he ever care to stay here. You and your ... friends ... are welcome to stay as well. Provided your dragon won't burn the house down." He laughed nervously, glancing at Audun.

Audun didn't seem to notice. He had picked up the mug in front of him and sniffed the contents. Annie noticed that he set it down again without drinking. She wondered what was in it. They couldn't be serving blood, could they?

Picking up her mug, Zoë took a sip, smiled appreciatively, then drained every drop. Francis picked his up, and without hesitating, drank it as well.

Annie thought about picking up hers, but the thought that it might be blood and that Francis was being uncommonly brave made her change her mind.

Audun stood up and stretched. "I doubt you have a bed big enough for me. I sleep in dragon form." He held up his hand to study his fingertips. Annie gasped when three of his nails turned into talons.

"We should leave now," Francis said, looking pointedly at Audun.

"Yes, we should," Zoë said, getting to her feet. She glanced at Corbin, who couldn't seem to take his horrified gaze off Audun. "I thank you for your hospitality and your offer of lodging, but we really can't stay. Our mission is urgent and we don't have much time."

"I understand," Corbin said, and hurried to the door. "Perhaps you'll be able to accompany your father on his next visit. We would be delighted to see you again."

"Perhaps Francis and I both will," Zoë said, and started out the door.

They were in the air again when Annie turned her head and said to Francis, "What happened back there? Do the vampires have a problem with you? I can understand why they would be afraid of Audun, with him being a dragon, but they didn't seem to like you, either."

"They don't like me and have made it very clear whenever we visit. I've been there a number of times with Zoë and her family, but they always pretend that they don't know who I am. I don't think they like that she married a human."

"But you're a prince and you use magic! You're also a very nice person," said Annie.

Francis shrugged. "That doesn't make any difference to them."

"Tell me, what exactly was in that pitcher? After Audun didn't drink his, I wondered if it was blood."

"I wouldn't put it past them," said Francis, "but it was just grape juice."

"I don't like juice," Audun told them. "And I don't like most vampires. Zoë and her family are the only ones I do like, but they aren't snobs like the rest. I can't stand people who think they're better than others, especially blood-sucking night crawlers who can't treat decent people with respect."

"I noticed that you didn't correct him when he thought you were a fire-breathing dragon," Annie told Audun.

"Most people can't tell the difference and I wasn't about to tell them otherwise. I don't care why they're afraid of me as long as they are."

"You do realize that we're going to be seeing more vampires on this trip," Annie warned him.

"Yes, I know," said Audun. "That doesn't mean I have to like them."

CHAPTER 10

THEY FLEW NORTHEAST under the starry sky for another few hours. "That looks like a good place to spend the night," Audun finally said, circling above a clearing in the forest. He landed then, the movement so smooth that Annie wasn't sure they had touched the ground until Francis started to get off.

"I don't mind sleeping in the forest, but why here instead of an inn?" asked Annie. "When you turned down the invitation to stay in Tottington, I thought you had someplace else in mind."

"Nope," Audun said as she climbed off his back. "Just someplace without vampires, present company excluded."

Zoë climbed out of Francis's pocket and fluttered to the ground. "I know," she said. "And I don't blame you. I don't like most vampires, either."

"I'm going to collect firewood," Francis told them. "Anyone want to go with me?"

"I will!" Zoë said. A moment later, she was a young woman holding her husband's hand as they walked off into the dark.

"Don't they need a light?" Annie asked.

"Zoë doesn't and Francis will make one if he wants it," said Audun. "I guess I'll make a fire pit. Humans seem to like having a fire at night and we don't want to burn down the entire forest."

While Audun scraped a circle in the ground with his talons, Annie collected rocks to edge the pit. By the time Zoë and Francis came back with kindling, the fire pit was ready for them. Francis used his magic to light the fire. He was standing in its light when he took an acorn out of the pouch on his belt. Annie was surprised when he twisted off the cap and pulled out three blankets.

"That's amazing!" Annie exclaimed. "What else do you have in there?"

"All sorts of stuff," Francis told her. "I got it at the Magic Marketplace ages ago."

"I need to get Liam a coronation gift. Do you think they still sell those acorns?" asked Annie.

Francis shrugged. "There's no telling. Aside from a few things that they always sell, like singing swords and bottomless tankards, the stuff there changes all

the time. Here, you can use this tonight," he said, handing a blanket to Annie.

When he tried to hand a blanket to Zoë, she shook her head, saying, "No thanks. I'm going to forage for a while, then I'll keep watch. There's no telling what lives in an unfamiliar forest, and someone has to watch over you. Audun can't because he needs to rest so he can fly tomorrow like he did today."

"I'll take a turn when you're ready to sleep," said Annie.

"You don't need to," Zoë told her. "I slept when I was in Francis's pocket and I'll sleep there tomorrow, too. Lie down and get some rest. You have another busy day ahead of you."

Annie was tired enough to welcome the suggestion. Spreading her blanket near the fire, she lay down and pulled the blanket around her. Audun had stayed in dragon form and was stretched out on the other side of the fire, already asleep. When Annie glanced their way, Francis and Zoë were talking quietly together. They kissed, then Francis lay down and Zoë turned into a bat. Annie closed her eyes as Zoë disappeared into the forest.

Certain that they would find Zoë's father soon and that he would be able to fix everything, Annie slept better than she had in a while. She woke abruptly a few hours later, however, when Zoë started screeching.

"Audun, Francis, wake up! I can't stop it and it's almost here!"

"What?" Francis said, scrambling out from under his blanket.

Audun was already on his feet, his great head swiveling from side to side as he gazed into the depths of the forest.

"I heard a sound and went to look," Zoë cried, fluttering around Francis. "It's a hydra and it's coming this way."

Francis was reaching for his sword when he said, "The fire probably attracted it. Stay back, Zoë. I'll handle this."

Darting toward Annie, Zoë turned into a girl again and hurried to stand beside her. Annie put her arm around the vampire girl's waist, and Zoë put an arm around hers so that they faced the hydra together.

"I hear it coming," said Audun. "It's a big one."

When Audun took a step toward the forest, Annie tried to peer past him, but it was too dark to see much of anything. And then she could hear it, too—a slithery, scraping sound that grew louder as it came their way. Branches snapped and trees shivered as the hydra drew closer. Although she had never seen a real hydra, she had seen their pictures in her father's book of mythological creatures. All she could remember now was that it was a snake and had more than one head.

Even so, she wasn't expecting the monster that emerged into the firelight. Its body was as big around as Audun's and each of the five heads was the size of a water barrel. Aside from the size, the heads were all very different. One had a rippled crest, another had drooping eyelids, a third had blubbery lips. The head in the middle had crossed eyes, while the one beside it looked vicious with a scar that angled across its face and horrible eyes that glared red.

"Who dares enter my forest without my permission?" the vicious-looking head said in a voice that even Annie could understand.

"Why do you always say that, Ssshomander?" asked the head with the crest. "No one ever asks your permission and you wouldn't give it if they did."

"Quiet, Sssilus," said Ssshomander. "You talk too much."

As the hydra advanced, Audun stepped in front of it, barring it from the clearing. Seeing a dragon blocking their way, the heads reared back and hissed. Coming from five separate throats, the sound was especially frightful.

"What is that?" said the head with blubbery lips. "Is that a dragon? You got me up in the middle of the night to challenge a dragon? Are you out of your mind?"

"Let's turn around and go back to bed now," said Sssilus. "I'm sleepy anyway."

"Yeah, back to bed," said the one with the crossed eyes.

The head with the droopy eyelids flared its nostrils and sniffed the air. "Something smells really good. It's been ages since we had a tasty bedtime snack. Why don't we start with that girl? I'd like to sink my fangs into her!"

It was hard to tell if the head was looking at Annie or Zoë, but they both stepped back at the same time.

"You can eat her," said Ssshomander. "After we take care of that dragon."

"Yeah, get the dragon," said the head with the crossed eyes.

"Why don't we just leave them alone?" Sssilus cried. "They aren't hurting anyone."

Ssshomander studied Audun for a moment. "This dragon must not have fire, or he would have flamed at us already. We'll take him down, then eat the humans."

"They look young to me; they should be easy to digest," the head with the droopy eyelids declared.

The hydra started toward them again with the head named Ssshomander weaving back and forth, hissing. When the head with the crossed eyes saw that, it started hissing and weaving, too. Francis stepped up beside Audun. Making a rolling motion with his hands, he created a ball of sparks, which he threw at the nasty head. The sparks exploded in the hydra's face, showering the heads on either side of it.

The hydra bellowed and began to move faster. When it was close enough, Ssshomander struck out at Francis. The young wizard danced aside even as he unsheathed his sword. Before Francis could wield Torrin, Audun stepped between his friend and the hydra. Spreading his wings, Audun stretched out his neck and roared in Ssshomander's face. The head reared back, then struck too fast for Annie to see. She did hear the sound of its fangs hitting Audun's scales, though, and the loud crack as the fangs shattered. When the hydra head pulled back, the tips of its fangs were broken off, leaving jagged stubs. In a flash, Audun lunged, sinking his own fangs into the creature's neck. The dragon shook the hydra's head until it screeched in a high, thin voice. The other heads joined in, begging for mercy.

Giving the head one final shake, Audun let go. The heads whimpered and drew back. With a last aggrieved hiss, the hydra turned and fled into the forest.

As soon as the hydra was gone, Audun turned to Francis, saying, "Why did you get involved? I was going to take care of this."

"I waited for you to breathe on it, but you didn't, so I thought I should step in," said Francis.

"You were too close," Audun told him. "I didn't want to risk hurting you with my poison gas."

"I suppose we should work out a system in case something like this ever happens again," Francis replied. "You'll just have to tell me how far away to stand."

"Uh, excuse me, but you two can discuss this later," Zoë interrupted. "I think we should find someplace else to sleep. I know that hydra heads grow back if they're cut off, so I wouldn't be surprised if their fangs do, too."

"I'm with Zoë," said Annie. "If there's any chance that the hydra might return, I'd like to be far away before it can come looking for us again."

"Fine by me," Audun told them. "I've already had all the sleep I need for tonight, and there are still plenty of hours before daylight. We can make real headway to our next stop if we leave now."

"Good," Francis said, scratching his side. "I'd rather not try to sleep here again anyway. I think I was lying on an ant hill."

༄

They flew for two more hours, landing only when Francis announced that he needed to use a shrub. When Audun set down, Annie was so tired that she fell asleep with her back against a tree while she waited for Francis. She woke long enough to hear that they would spend the rest of the night there and was asleep again in moments.

Annie woke, groggy, when Francis declared in a loud voice, "What do you mean Zoë's not here?"

The sun was peeping over the horizon, bathing the landscape in otherworldly light. They had slept on the boundary between forest and farmland with hay growing in a field only yards away. Swallows dipped and soared over the hay while butterflies fluttered from flower to flower.

"She went foraging a few hours ago and hasn't come back yet," explained Audun. "I told her I'd keep watch, but I didn't expect her to be gone this long."

"Do you know which way she went?" Francis asked.

"That way," Audun said, pointing toward the field.

Francis frowned as he gazed across the field. "We have to go look for her. Something must have happened to keep her from coming back before now." Taking the acorn out of the pouch, he twisted off the cap and took out the black dragon scale. He muttered under his breath, turning the scale until it flashed red.

When Francis started walking, Annie scrambled to her feet to follow him. Before stepping into the hayfield, she glanced back at Audun. In the few seconds she'd been looking the other way, he had changed back into a human. She found the sudden change a little disconcerting. "I don't know if I'll ever get used to that," she murmured to herself.

The hay was waist high and the ground beneath it uneven, so Annie had to give each footstep her fullest attention. Birds shot out of the hay at their approach, and a rabbit suddenly bounded away in front of her, making her heart pound and her thoughts turn to whatever else the tall grasses might hide. She was relieved when they finally reached a country lane and Francis started down it.

They hadn't gone far before they spotted a barn and a small cottage. A little farther and they could hear someone shouting over the barking of dogs. "That's it, boys! Tell the wee beastie who's boss around here."

Annie hurried to walk beside Francis. She glanced at the dragon scale. It was glowing red and was aimed directly at the spot between the cottage and the barn.

Francis looked grim as they came in sight of the farmer and his dogs. The man was holding a big stick, watching while two dogs barked and lunged at something small and dark caught in a net strung between two poles. When the dogs backed off for a moment, the man swung his stick at the net, hitting it so that it swayed and bobbed. The little creature inside it cried out.

Suddenly Francis was grabbing the stick from the man's hand and tossing it aside. When the man turned around, Francis punched him in the nose, knocking him to the ground. The dogs went wild, snapping at Francis until Audun stepped up. With one deep-throated growl from the dragon-turned-man, the dogs took off running.

"What did you do that for?" the farmer said, looking up at Francis accusingly. Blood streamed from the man's nose, and he wiped at it with the back of his hand, smearing it across his face.

"You were trying to hit my wife!" Francis declared. Giving the farmer a disgusted look, he took hold of the net, gently untangling it from the shivering, whimpering bat. Annie could see now that it was Zoë, who looked more frightened than hurt. When she noticed that Francis was so mad that his hands shook, she hurried to help.

The farmer was getting to his feet when Francis and Annie finally freed Zoë. Francis gently set her on the ground, where she immediately turned back into a human-looking girl and collapsed into her husband's arms.

"I knew she was a vampire and not just an ordinary bat!" the farmer exclaimed. "Why didn't she turn to ash when the sun came out like all the others?"

"She's only half vampire, you fool," said Francis. "She doesn't even look like a vampire bat. What's wrong with you?"

"I...I didn't know," the farmer stammered. "I put out that net every night to catch the vampire bats. They come to suck the blood from my milk cow. Putting her in the barn for the night isn't good enough. They get in even when the door's shut; there are so many gaps between the boards that there's no keeping them out. The old girl is really suffering. When I get up in the morning, I leave the bats in the net and they turn to ash when sunlight touches 'em. I've never had one stay alive like this before. I'm sorry it was your wife, but if she was here to suck the blood from my cow, she deserved what she got."

"I was catching insects!" said Zoë. "I don't drink anyone's blood!"

"Maybe you don't, but the vampires from over the hills do. They come here two or three times a week, or at least they did before I put out my net. Those monsters don't have any respect for other people's animals. They think they're so high and mighty living in their fancy house with their evil ways. No one dares go in their valley, but I figure the vampires are fair game if they come to my farm."

"They're just over those hills, huh?" said Francis. "Is their home called Heartsblood Manor?"

"You've heard of it? I knew word of a place as bad as that would get around!" the farmer said.

"Actually, we're on our way there now," Francis told him. "I didn't realize we were so close."

The farmer looked around nervously before leaning toward Francis and whispering, "You won't tell them about the nets, will you? I'm just trying to defend my livelihood the best way I know how. If you tell the vampires what I've done, they'll come here to suck me dry, and then where will my family be?"

"We won't tell them," said Francis. "But I think you

should put your nets away. The vampires are bound to catch on if you keep trapping them."

§

Annie was glad to get away from the worried farmer, but she wasn't so sure she wanted to visit such frightening vampires. As Audun skimmed the tops of the trees, she wondered if the vampires would be more like the ones who refused to leave Treecrest, or the marginally nicer ones in Tottington. Either way, she couldn't wait to find Zoë's father so their trip could be over.

Leaving the hills behind, they came upon a valley filled with dense forest and alive with birdsong. When Audun spotted a house as big as a castle but without turrets or a moat, he circled it and began his descent.

Annie looked around warily, even though she knew that the vampires would be asleep. The manor house seemed bigger as they neared it, and the gardens around it more extensive. Although everything was trimmed and in good repair, the place looked empty and abandoned without a single person in sight.

After circling the house and grounds one more time, Audun landed in a particularly lovely garden. "We might as well spend the day here," he said as Francis helped Annie climb off. "We won't be able to talk to anyone until nightfall."

115

"Do you think your parents might be here?" Annie asked Zoë.

"I doubt it," Zoë replied. "They never stay long in any one place and this would have been their second stop. I didn't want to skip it, though, just in case they'd decided to stay for a few days."

"I don't suppose we could go in the house and look for them?" Annie said, sounding hopeful.

Zoë looked shocked. "I wouldn't dream of it! You wouldn't want strangers wandering through your house uninvited. Besides, you'd be putting yourself in great danger. Just because vampires sleep during the day doesn't mean they aren't protected. I don't know what Count Bracken does, but my father pays some very nasty creatures to guard his castle while we sleep. I wouldn't dare go in the count's home without a personal invitation at the door. We're safe now provided we stay in the garden and don't go anywhere near the house."

CHAPTER 11

ANNIE THOUGHT THE GARDEN might be the prettiest one she had ever seen, or it would have been if the buds had been open. "I love the fountain and the arbors hiding those lovely benches, but none of the flowers are actually blooming," Annie said after they'd explored every inch of it. "Don't you think it's strange that not a single blossom is open?"

"During one of my visits here with my parents, the gardener told me that he'd planted only night-blooming flowers in this garden," Zoë told her. "The vampires who live at Heartsblood want to be able to see them."

"If the gardener is a vampire, he must work at night," said Annie. "Doesn't that make it harder for him?"

Zoë shrugged. "Vampires can see perfectly well in the dark."

"That's why they can sneak up on you so easily,"

Francis told her. "Zoë likes to jump out and startle me at night sometimes."

"I can't help it," Zoë said, laughing. "The expression on your face is always priceless!"

Audun raised his head to look at them. He had stayed a dragon, and had been napping in the sun for the last few hours. "If you don't mind, I might do a little hunting before nightfall. If I catch something now, it would give me time to digest before we leave."

"You can hunt, just not in this valley," said Zoë. "If the vampires were going to farms outside the valley to feed, the count must reserve all the animals in the valley for himself. He'd be angry if he learned that some were missing."

"Then I might be gone a little longer," said Audun. "I don't want to eat any of the farmer's livestock, either, so I'll have to look farther afield."

"Please don't be gone too long," Annie said. "After all the things I've heard, I don't want to stay here any longer than is absolutely necessary."

With Audun gone and Zoë having a private conversation with Francis, Annie found a deep-seated garden bench in the shade and curled up on it for a nap. It was dusk when she woke and went looking for her friends. Seeing Audun land at the other end of the garden, she hurried down the path to join him. Zoë and Francis were already there.

"We can head to the house now," Zoë said when she

saw Annie. "Everyone should be up and about by the time we knock on the door."

Zoë led the way with her hand on her husband's arm. Annie was happy to take Audun's arm when he offered it to her; having a dragon so close made her feel safer and gave her the confidence to follow Zoë up the steps to the wide front door.

Francis knocked on the door. Seconds later, a vampire servant in fine livery opened it. "We have come to see Count Bracken," Zoë announced.

The vampire recognized her right away. His eyes grew wide and he gestured to something behind him. Although it was dark inside, some places looked even darker than others. There was a whisper of sound and the darkness behind him shifted. Annie had a feeling that something was watching them. The servant glanced back and gestured again. Black on black roiled, and the unseen presence was gone.

"It's awfully dark in there," Annie said to her friends.

The servant bowed and opened the door wider. "You grace us with your visit, Your Highness," he said. "Please enter."

Annie panicked at the thought of stepping into the darkened room, where the very air looked threatening. She glanced at Audun, who patted her hand and smiled reassuringly.

Zoë stepped inside and looked around. "Lights would be nice," she said.

The servant gestured again and candles flared in a chandelier above them, in wall sconces around the room, and on every table in the hall. Suddenly the space was bright and far more welcoming. Annie appreciated Zoë's thoughtfulness, knowing that the vampire girl didn't need the light herself.

Audun pressed Annie's arm against his side as they stepped across the threshold. The room was beautiful, with a high ceiling and a patterned stone floor. Tables bearing candles and bouquets of flowers stood against the walls, which were decorated with shields both modern and very, very old. Regardless, Annie couldn't help being repulsed by the odor of mustiness and freshly turned soil that permeated the room. It reminded her too much of the smell they'd encountered in the house in Tottington. She glanced up at the ceiling, half expecting to see bats hanging upside down above them.

"Please, follow me," said the servant, and led the way to a room down a short corridor.

Candles flared and the logs in a large fireplace lit themselves as Annie and her friends filed in. The room was elegant, with tapestries on the walls and fresh flowers on the tables, but Annie still felt uneasy. After they'd seated themselves on the cushioned benches and comfortable-looking chairs, the servant turned to Zoë, saying, "Grunwald will be with you shortly." He left, closing the door behind him, but even then Annie felt as if someone or something was in the room with her and her friends.

"Do you feel it?" she asked Audun, who was seated beside her. "There's something else in the room besides us."

Audun looked around. He shook his head, saying, "I don't see anything. But don't worry; nothing will hurt you with me here."

The door opened and a man walked in. Tall and thin with a hawk-like nose, he didn't seem to see anyone but Zoë. He looked so aristocratic that Annie was sure he had to be the count.

"Your Highness," he said, bowing low. "How wonderful to see you again. I understand you've come to call upon Count Bracken. I'm afraid you've missed him by a few days. He left shortly after your father's visit and has yet to return. He'll be very sorry that he didn't get to see you."

"Then perhaps you might be able to tell me if my father mentioned where he and my mother were going next."

"I believe he said that they were on their way to Highcliff Castle," said the man. "May I be so presumptuous as to invite you to stay for dinner with the family? As you may recall, Count Bracken's mother, aunt, and brothers reside here. I am sure they would be delighted to have you dine with them."

"It would give me great pleasure to see them again,"

Zoë replied. "There will be four of us joining them." She looked pointedly at each of her friends, then pretended not to see the look of dismay on the man's face.

"Very good," the man said, his words sounding forced. "Dinner will be served shortly."

As soon as the door shut behind him, Zoë turned to her friends and said, "I'm sorry. I hadn't intended to stay, but there was no polite way to get out of it."

"Why did you have to tell him how many of us there would be?" asked Annie. "Couldn't he see that for himself?"

"If it had been up to him, I would have been the only one to be seated with the count's family. Most vampires don't regard non-vampires as people and capable of conversation."

"They think of us the way some people think of dogs. Useful at times, but not worthy of eating at the table with them," said Francis. "The only humans they like are the ones they've turned, although even turned humans aren't considered to be on the same level as vampires born to vampires."

Something shifted in the back of the room and Annie heard the faintest of sounds, but when she looked, there was nothing there. Whatever it was, she couldn't wait to leave this place.

A servant girl came to the door a short time later, offering Zoë a chance to "refresh herself and change her clothes." The vampire princess declined the offer.

When the girl was gone, Zoë told Annie, "I want to be able to leave right after we eat and I have no desire to travel dressed in the overdone clothes they wear to dinner here. You'll see what I mean."

They all stood when another servant came to announce that dinner was about to be served. When Annie entered the dining room with her friends, she felt decidedly underdressed. Her plain traveling clothes looked shabby beside the elegant gowns the two vampire women wore. One was dressed all in silver with beading and bows everywhere. The other's gown was a deep, dark red, the color of old blood. Annie thought that the black-and-gray embroidery made it look like rotting meat. She could understand why Zoë wouldn't want to dress like them.

Zoë, however, managed to make the women look overdressed when she held her head high and acted as if she were in charge. Taking a cue from her friend, Annie ignored the women's disdainful looks when their gaze passed over her.

The four vampires in the room all appeared to be in their twenties, but Annie remembered the steward saying that one of the women was the count's aunt and the other was his mother. Apparently, vampires didn't age the same way as humans. While the servant led Zoë to the head of the table, her husband and friends were left to find their own seats. Annie ended up sitting between Audun and one of the count's brothers.

Francis was at the end next to the other brother, who looked surly and not at all happy to be there.

The two vampire women spoke only to Zoë, telling her how lovely she looked and how well her father had seemed when he stopped by. Although Zoë kept up a lively conversation with them, Annie didn't hear much of it because the vampire man beside her never stopped talking.

"You and that one," he said, pointing at Francis, "are the first humans we've ever had here who came voluntarily. I wonder why our princess is traveling with your kind. There must be something special about you. I wonder what it is."

He took a sip of something in his chalice that left a thick, red droplet on the corner of his lips. Annie looked away.

"Bracken isn't here right now. He went to visit a friend and has yet to return," said the vampire. "He does that quite often, actually. There's no saying when he'll be back. Mother doesn't like it when he's gone so long, but she doesn't tell him that."

Annie wondered if the count was one of the vampires still at her parents' castle.

A servant offered her a platter of meat. Annie shuddered when she saw that it was raw and still bleeding. "No, thank you," she said, shaking her head.

The man next to her took a large portion. "I'm Rance and my brother is Spenser. I don't mind humans, but

Spenser hates them, especially now. His best friend flew off the other night to feed and never came back. Spenser is convinced that a human killed him, but he doesn't know where or how. I almost feel sorry for whoever did it if my brother ever finds him."

Annie was grateful that another servant brought a platter of vegetables just then so she had a reason to turn away. A picture of the farmer's nets had popped into her head and she was afraid that the vampire could see from her expression that she knew something about missing vampires. After helping herself to squash and carrots, she ate a few bites. She noticed that Rance waved the platter away without taking any.

"See how my mother is fawning over the princess?" said the vampire. "She hopes that Zoë will fall for Bracken and want to marry him someday. She's been dreaming about the match for years."

"But Zoë is already married to Francis," Annie protested.

"That human?" said Rance, glancing down the table at Francis. "He doesn't count. Humans don't live long enough to matter. Give the princess enough decades and she'll be ready for Bracken. I wouldn't mind having royalty in the family. It certainly would make Mother happy."

Annie glanced at the two women talking to Zoë. Something moved behind them, but when she looked directly at the spot, there was nothing there.

"Tell me, Your Highness," one of the vampire woman trilled. "What of your companions? I know that human male is your husband, but tell me about the girl. Is she your blood donor?"

Annie paled when she realized that the woman was talking about her. The vampires all turned to look her way and she almost dropped the knife she was using to cut up her carrots.

"No, she is not," Zoë said, sounding angry. "She is my friend and a princess in her own kingdom."

"You have human friends?" said the other woman. "Well, of course you do. After all, you are married to one!"

"And what about that lovely young man with all that gorgeous white hair?" the first woman said, looking at Audun. "Is he your blood donor or another friend?"

"What is he exactly? He smells delicious," Rance said, leaning past Annie to sniff the air. "Hot and spicy. I wonder what his blood tastes like."

"He's my friend," said Zoë. "And I wouldn't try to find out what he tastes like if I were you. He bites. Dragons do, you know."

Rance drew back, dismay plain on his face. His brother stared at Audun as if he couldn't quite believe what he'd heard.

Annie stopped pretending to be interested in the food in front of her. Setting her knife on her trencher, she sat farther back in her chair and glanced at Audun.

The dragon-turned-man seemed as calm as ever, but Annie saw the tightness around his mouth and that his eyes didn't look fully human anymore.

Zoë must have noticed it as well, because she got to her feet, saying, "I believe it's time for us to go. Annie, Audun, please wait for me in the corridor. I'd like to say a few words to our hosts."

Audun stood quickly and pulled Annie's chair back for her. The vampires were all watching Zoë as she took a long, slow sip from a chalice while Francis hurried to stand by her chair. Annie walked from the room with her back straight and her head held high. She doubted that any of the vampires even noticed that she had gone, but it rankled that they thought of humans as no more than dogs. They obviously didn't even consider them worthy of common courtesy. Imagine— talking about her as if she were there so someone could drink her blood! She was glad they were afraid of Audun.

Annie was halfway down the corridor when she turned to say something to her dragon friend. She'd thought he had followed her out the door, but instead she could see him in the doorway, waiting for Francis and Zoë. She was about to start back when she felt something cold on her cheek. Spinning on her heel, she turned to look around, but no one was there. When something whispered and moved beside her, she turned again and felt a clammy touch on her wrist.

127

"Now cut that out!" she exclaimed. "I know you're there, whatever you are!"

Suddenly Annie felt as if she were surrounded. The air seemed to seethe around her, and she heard a murmuring that almost sounded like words. She swatted her hand as if at an insect, but all she felt was emptiness.

Then Zoë, Francis, and Audun were beside her. "Is something wrong?" asked Zoë.

"I don't know what it is, but I keep seeing something, although I don't really see it, if you know what I mean," Annie said.

"I see it now, too," Audun told her. His eyes were fully dragon, and he was staring intently at a spot just past Annie's shoulder.

As Annie watched, the invisible nothings started to become slightly more discernable, taking on vaguely human forms. "Are they vampires?" Annie asked Zoë. "Were they using their magic to stay invisible?"

Zoë shook her head. "No, these are wraiths. I've heard about them, but I've never encountered any before. They seem to want something of you, Annie."

The wraiths were clustered around Annie, watching her with mournful-looking eyes. Aside from the impression of a head and face, they seemed to be nothing more than barely visible tattered rags that fluttered around an unseen body. The closest wraiths reached out to Annie, touching her with almost imperceptible hands. When one touched her arm, Annie could swear she heard it say, "Help us!"

"I think I know what they want," Zoë said. "We have to go right now."

"What *do* they want?" Annie asked her. "Is there something I can do to help them?"

Grabbing Annie by the hand, Zoë told her, "You can run!"

The wraiths were pressing closer to Annie when she started running. Fearing that they might want something dreadful from her, Annie ran as fast as she could. As she approached the door, she felt pinpricks of cold as they collided with her from behind. And then Annie and her friends were outside and the wraiths were, too, dozens of them bursting out of the manor with such force that she could feel them bumping into her and almost knocking her off her feet. Francis, Zoë, and Audun watched with Annie as the wraiths swirled around them, then disappeared into the night sky.

"What just happened?" asked Francis.

"I'm not exactly certain," said Zoë, "but I think Annie just released some creatures who had been kept here against their will for a very long time. Remember how I told you that my father pays beasts to guard his castle? I've heard that vampires used wraiths as unpaid guards long ago, but I didn't know that anyone still did. If I'm right, the wraiths were brought here to guard the manor house and were never allowed to leave. Vampire magic couldn't keep them here, so someone must have used some very old magic to imprison them. Annie's presence must have weakened the magic enough for the wraiths to escape."

"I think you're right," Annie told her. "Just before they flew off, I was sure I heard someone say, 'Thank you!'"

"We need to go," Audun said as he stepped away from the house. A moment later he was a dragon, gleaming white in the light still pouring through the door of the manor house. "After what you said inside, and after Annie released their guards, those vampires are not going to be very happy with us. I, for one, don't want to stick around to see what they do."

"What did you say to them, Zoë?" Annie asked as she climbed onto Audun's back.

"Just that I thought they had been rude to my friends and they had no right to treat you that way," replied Zoë. "I told them that they needed some lessons in civility and that it would be a very long time before I visited there again, if ever."

Francis was settling down behind Annie when he laughed and said, "In other words, she gave them a good scolding." He opened his pocket and Zoë the bat slipped inside.

"They must be terribly disappointed," Annie said as Audun took off. "Rance told me that his family hoped

Zoë would marry the count someday. Apparently, humans aren't good enough for vampires."

"Those vampires aren't good enough for anyone!" Zoë said, her voice muffled. "And I'll be sure to tell my father exactly what happened!"

CHAPTER 12

HIGHCLIFF CASTLE WAS only a few hours away by dragon-back, so it was still night when they finally arrived. Located on a cliff overlooking the ocean, the castle was unreachable from the land on three sides. On the fourth side, the curtain wall towered above anyone approaching, and the imposing gatehouse with multiple holes through which defenders could drop boulders would be enough to frighten away anyone but the bravest. With its high wall towers, and large bailey surrounding the keep, it looked more like a military installation than a home.

After circling the castle, Audun swooped low over the empty field that was the bailey, startling bats that darted into the night. Even before they landed, Annie smelled something awful. She crinkled her nose in distaste and asked Francis, "What is that awful smell?"

"Harpies," said Francis. "They stink more than

anything else in the world. I hate coming here because of the stench, but if Zoë comes here, so do I. Vampires' sense of smell isn't very good, so it doesn't bother them. The duke has harpies guard the area around the castle during the day. It's a super-effective deterrent against intruders."

"Are they here at night, too?" Annie asked, looking warily around as Audun landed.

"No, they're off doing their own thing. They'll be back at daybreak, though."

Annie looked around as she climbed off the dragon's back. Torches were placed at intervals around the walls, but they weren't nearly enough to illuminate such a big space. What she could see of the castle was daunting, however; she really, *really* hoped they'd find Garrid and could leave before dawn.

As Francis dismounted, Zoë crawled out of his pocket and fluttered to the ground. The sound of a woman screaming made Annie gasp and look around. In an instant, Francis had his sword drawn and was running in the direction of the screams. Audun launched himself into the air and soon passed Francis. The dragon circled above the bailey near the curtain wall, then flew back to land beside Francis. Annie peered into the sparsely lit bailey, trying to see what was making the terrible sound. She couldn't understand why Francis and Audun started back, even after the woman screamed again.

"It's a screeching peacock," Francis told the girls as he got closer. "It sure had me fooled. I could have sworn it was a woman in terrible danger."

"I thought so, too," said Audun.

"I don't know why anyone keeps those birds," Annie declared. "Their feathers are pretty, but they sound awful." Her nerves were still jangling when she turned toward the keep door. Somehow, she didn't think things were going to be any less frightening inside.

"I'm not turning human all the way this time," Audun told them as he started to change. "Sometimes dragon senses can be very useful when I'm in human form."

The four friends drew closer together as they approached the keep. Torches on either side of the door showed the way. There were no guards by the door, so Francis stepped up and knocked. They waited, but no one came.

"I'll try," said Audun. He knocked hard enough to shake the heavy door, but there was still no response.

"The castle isn't abandoned, is it?" asked Annie. "Maybe no one's here."

"Someone is here, all right," said Audun. "I can hear them inside."

"You can hear them?" Annie said in surprise. "I can't hear a thing through that door."

"Dragons have excellent hearing," Audun declared.

"Maybe I should just open it," suggested Francis.

Audun shook his head. "I should be the one..."

"Oh, for goodness' sake. We'll stand here all night if we don't just do something!" Annie said, and opened the door herself.

Although she didn't push it very far, it opened the rest of the way on its own, revealing a feebly lit corridor beyond. A cold breeze blew from the corridor, carrying with it the scent of freshly turned soil. Annie froze when two glowing red eyes seemed to materialize out of the dark. Something emerged from the shadows, growling deep in its throat. Annie stepped back as a black dog as big as a calf stepped into the torchlight.

Zoë stepped forward and announced in a voice that demanded attention, "I am Her Royal Highness Princess Zoë. I order you to stop this immediately."

It looked as if the dog were dissolving into the darkness behind it. When it was gone, a meek-looking man dressed as a servant stood there, bowing to the princess. "I'm so sorry, Your Highness. I wasn't sure what to do when you knocked. I'm not usually the one to answer the door, you see, but with all the confusion it somehow fell to me to see who was here and, well, I do apologize."

"Was that one of those illusions you told me about?" Annie asked her friend.

Zoë nodded, but when she spoke it was to the servant. "I have come to see the duke."

"He isn't here," said the man. "We heard he's dead

135

and no one quite knows what to do. Vampires don't die very often."

"Then I would like to speak to whoever is in charge," Zoë told him.

"That would be, uh, just a moment please," the man said, and turned to someone behind him. "Finley, stop hiding in the shadows and come help me."

After a moment's hesitation, a bat fluttered into the torchlight and landed beside the man. He turned into another servant who looked even meeker than the first.

"This is Her Royal Highness Princess Zoë. She wants to speak to whoever is in charge, but I don't know who that is. Do you?"

Finley ducked his head and said, "That'd be Dexter, wouldn't it, Deelio?"

"He's the steward, but he's not in charge of everything," said Deelio. "I was thinking more like Lord Reynard. His friend Maganen claims that Reynard is the new duke."

Annie glanced at her friends. Reynard was here without the duke. That could mean all sorts of things.

"We're not sure who is in charge at the moment," Deelio told Zoë. "The duke never designated an heir, but then why would he? We all expected him to live a lot longer. If you wouldn't mind waiting a minute, we'll go find out."

He was closing the door when Audun set his hand

on it and pushed. "Why don't you invite us in while you inquire?"

"Oh, of course!" Deelio said. "Please come in."

When Francis stepped forward to walk beside Zoë with his hand on the hilt of his sword, Annie dropped back to join Audun, glad that he was with them. All four of them walked with their heads turning from side to side, peering into the dark corners and down the long corridor. The few lit torches did little to dispel the gloom and Annie thought it was the darkest and ugliest castle she had ever seen.

Sad, haunting music came from somewhere up ahead. The cool breeze caressed their faces and made Annie shiver. Bats darted above them, some coming so close that Annie could feel the brush of their wings. She was startled when Audun stopped walking suddenly, and she turned to see why. He stood outside a closed door, sniffing the air. When he turned back, he looked puzzled.

A little farther down the corridor, they reached the doorway to the great hall. The music was louder now, and sounded even more mournful. Annie couldn't see how large the room was because the guttering torches on the walls were few and far between. The ceiling was higher, though, and the bats no longer came so close. "You may wait here," Deelio told them, gesturing into the hall. A moment later, he and Finley were bats fluttering down the corridor.

Although Annie could just make out dark forms nearby and had the impression that there were many people in the hall, the only thing she could hear was the music. The lighting was so poor that she couldn't see very well, either. "I wish I could see better," she whispered to her friends.

"I would ask someone if we could have more light, but I wouldn't know who to talk to," said Zoë. "I guess it's up to me." With a flick of her hand, every torch on the wall, every candle on the tables, and every log in the enormous fireplaces at both ends of the hall lit themselves.

The hall was bright enough now that Annie could see vampires seated around the tables blinking at the sudden light. Most of the vampires close to them were dressed as servants, while a few clusters of lesser nobles were seated throughout the room. They all remained silent as they watched Annie and her friends come farther into the hall.

"We might as well sit down," said Zoë, gesturing to the nearest empty table.

"Maybe we should leave," Annie whispered to her friends. "I don't like the way those vampires are looking at us."

"We're not going anywhere until we find out what happened to my parents," Zoë whispered back, and led the way to the table.

Annie tried not to be too obvious when she turned

to look at the vampires. One of them was strolling between the tables, playing a lute and singing. Some were talking to their neighbors, while others played games of dice. Almost all had mugs in front of them. Annie wondered what they were drinking until Audun leaned toward her and said, "Yes, they are drinking blood. I can smell it from here." He sniffed the air and added, "It smells old and stale."

Zoë nodded. "Vampires find stale blood intoxicating. I believe the duke stores it in wine barrels in the cellar. A lot of these vampires are already drunk, which means they're bound to be even more dangerous right now. It seems that they aren't mourning their duke as much as enjoying the chance to do whatever they please."

The music grew louder as the lute-playing vampire approached their table. Even when the man wasn't singing, the song he played made Annie feel like crying. "Can't you play something cheerful?" she asked when he paused behind her.

"These are the only songs I know," the vampire said, and walked on.

Vampires walked past the table on their way to refill their mugs. When any of them passed her, Annie edged as far from them as she could get. One bumped into Audun and the dragon-turned-man looked back to glare at him. Just then, Annie felt a featherlight touch on her neck and shrieked when she realized that a

139

vampire was preparing to bite her. She jumped up, trying to push the vampire away.

"Leave her alone!" Francis cried, drawing his sword as he got to his feet.

Then Audun was standing as well. With one shove, he pushed the vampire so hard that the man flew backward over the next table.

"This place is awful," said Annie. "The people are awful, the hall is as cold as a tomb, and there aren't any tapestries on the walls or rushes on the floor—nothing that makes a castle comfortable."

"The duke must not value such things," Francis said with a shrug.

When Annie glanced toward the door, she saw a bat flutter into the room and head straight for their table. The moment the bat landed, he turned into the human-looking Deelio. "Please come with me, Your Highness," he said, bowing.

Zoë got to her feet first and led her friends from the great hall. They followed the servant down the corridor and up two flights of stairs to a closed door. Deelio knocked. When a voice called, "You may enter," he opened the door and stuck his head in.

"Her Royal Highness Princess Zoë," he announced, then opened the door wide enough to let Zoë and her friends in.

Three vampires were seated at a long table and they turned as one to face Zoë. Although the short, stout vampire wearing a steward's medallion was unfamiliar, Annie recognized the vampires dressed as nobles. The more handsome of the two was the duke's rude nephew, Reynard. The one with the wide-set eyes had been among the dancers in her parents' great hall.

"You returned from Treecrest," said Zoë. "Did everyone leave?"

"No, just us," said Reynard. "We were the smart ones. The rest are still there, fighting the good fight."

"I see," said Zoë. "I've come to speak to the duke, but I've been told that he's dead."

"That's right!" said the other noble. "Quite dead. Some humans killed him in a faraway kingdom, as you well know."

"He wasn't dead when I saw him last," Zoë told him.

"He is now," said Reynard. "As his nephew, I'm the new duke and I'm in charge here."

"Then I'm sure you're very busy taking over for your uncle," said Zoë. "I just want to know if my father came by and when he left if he was here."

The vampire who Annie guessed had to be Reynard's friend Maganen spoke up. "Prince Garrid was here days ago, but he didn't stay. He left when we told him what had happened to the duke." Annie thought it was odd that he looked above Zoë and not directly at her.

When she glanced at the steward, he looked smug, but she noticed that he was fiddling with his medallion.

141

"I didn't expect to see you here," Reynard said to Zoë as he gave her an appraising look. "I wonder why you would need your father so badly that you would come all the way to Highcliff to find him. And your little human friend is a real surprise. It's quite a shame—such a long journey only to be disappointed at the end."

A bell tolled somewhere in the castle and Lord Reynard turned to the steward. "Please show our guests to rooms where they may spend the day. Dawn will be upon us soon and Princess Zoë cannot leave until nightfall. The princess may stay in the royal suite."

"But I don't—" Zoë began.

"We'll have much to discuss come evening, dear Princess. I insist that you accept the castle's hospitality," Reynard told her.

"You can't just—"

"Ah, but I can," said Reynard. "You're in my castle and I'm in charge here."

The steward rose from his seat to open the door. He ushered them into the corridor, where they found vampires dressed as guards waiting for them. "If you will come this way, we'll see that you have the appropriate accommodations," Dexter said to Zoë.

"My husband goes with me," Zoë told the steward.

"Of course, Your Highness," he said, and gave her an ingratiating smile.

They had started down the corridor when Audun appeared to drop a coin. They all waited while he looked for it, but finding the coin seemed to take a very long time. When a guard nudged him, Audun stood and started walking again, but he didn't look happy.

The steward and the guards took Annie and her friends down one corridor after another. When they finally stopped, Dexter opened a door and gestured to Annie, saying, "You will stay in this room today."

Annie didn't want to go anywhere in the castle without her friends. "But I thought we were staying together," she said, sounding distressed.

"She's right," said Zoë. "We want to share one room."

"The other rooms are just down the corridor, Your Highness," Dexter announced. "You will be more comfortable with your own accommodations."

Annie was about to protest when two of the guards took her by her arms and half walked, half dragged her into the room. Audun and Francis made as if to go after her, but Zoë shook her head, saying, "It's all right, Annie. It's almost dawn."

Annie watched helplessly as the vampires shut her in the room by herself. She waited until she could no longer hear footsteps before trying the door and wasn't surprised to find that they had locked it. What had Zoë meant when she said it was almost dawn? Were the vampires going to sleep soon and would they leave her alone? Was Zoë telling her that her friends would come rescue her at daybreak? Either way, Annie wished she knew what was going to happen.

Wrapping her arms around her body for warmth and comfort, Annie studied the room. It was cold and dark with only one lit candle on a small table by the bed. A large, dark chest took up one corner. There was also a table beside a small wooden bench. Since it was supposedly almost dawn, she started looking for a window. It took her some time to locate one, but it was boarded over and the boards were too securely attached to remove.

Tired and dispirited, Annie sat on the edge of the bed. It was comfortable and the covers offered the only warmth in the room. The castle was silent, so she assumed that morning had come and the vampires had gone to sleep. Burrowing under the covers, she lay down, determined to stay awake. But in only a matter of minutes she, too, was asleep.

CHAPTER 13

A BARELY AUDIBLE SOUND in the room woke Annie. She lay there, listening, but didn't hear anything else. The still-burning candle was nearly as tall as it had been before she fell asleep, so she knew she hadn't been asleep for long. She closed her eyes, her body tense beneath the covers, wondering if she should get up and try to pry the boards off the window.

The mattress moved as if someone had bumped it and Annie felt something cold on her neck. She lurched upright, screaming as loud as she could. The vampire who was leaning over her looked startled. When she pulled her arm back and punched him in the nose with all her might, he fell to the floor, wailing.

Annie jumped out of bed and turned to face the vampire. It was Reynard's friend Maganen. He looked younger now than he had sitting at the table with Reynard and Dexter, but Annie knew that didn't mean anything with vampires. Touching his nose gingerly with one hand, he glared up at Annie and said, "You hit me!"

"You were trying to bite my neck!" Annie replied.

"You were supposed to be asleep. If you were, you wouldn't have felt a thing. I'm surprised the magic in that bed didn't work. It always has in the past. A witch placed a very good spell on it years ago."

"Witches' magic doesn't work on me," said Annie. "How did you get in?"

"Through the secret passage," he said, wincing when he touched the bump forming on his nose. "I think you broke it!"

"The passage?" asked Annie.

"No! My nose! Now I won't be nearly so handsome," he said with a sob.

"Some girls find men with broken noses ruggedly handsome," she said without really thinking. "I need to go."

"You're supposed to stay here," the vampire said, getting to his feet.

"Why, so you can try to bite me again? I don't think so!"

Suddenly the door burst into flames. Within seconds it had turned to ash and a blue-and-white dragon began to force his way through the opening that was much too small. As the door frame cracked and split apart, the wall around it crumbled.

"Are you all right?" Audun said as he came into the room.

"We heard you screaming," said Francis as he walked in behind Audun.

"Maganen tried to bite my neck!" Annie said, pointing.

"Is that a real dragon?" the vampire asked in a hoarse whisper.

"Yes, and he's a friend of mine, so you'll stay out of our way if you know what's good for you," Annie told him.

The bell tolled somewhere in the castle again and Maganen gasped. "It's dawn!" he cried. In an instant, he had changed into a bat and fled to the darkest corner of the room.

Annie got out of the way as Audun started turning around. "Did you rescue Francis, too?" she asked him.

"He most certainly did not!" Francis said, avoiding Audun's tail. "I'd been locked in a room down the hall from his. I used my magic to get out, then let him out, too. We were on our way here to unlock your door when we heard you scream. You have excellent lungs, by the way. You were really quite loud. We thought you were being attacked, so I got a spell ready and Audun turned into his dragon self."

"A vampire trying to bite one's neck inspires volume," Annie replied. "What about Zoë?"

"We were going to rescue her last," said Francis. "Tell Annie what you told me, Audun."

147

Audun's foot had gotten wedged under the bed. He grunted as he pulled it out, cracking the leg of the bed so it sagged on one side. "When I dropped a coin outside Reynard's door, I did it so I could hear what he was saying to his friend," said Audun. "Maganen was telling Reynard that Zoë had shown up at the perfect time. They could kill you, me, and Francis, then Reynard could marry Zoë, even if she wasn't a full-blood and he didn't love her. Being married to the princess would make his claim to the dukedom stronger."

"They won't bother Zoë until they get rid of us," Francis told her.

"Do you know where she is?" Annie asked.

"Just down the hall," said Audun. "I can smell her."

Audun made an even larger hole on his way out of the room. As Annie stepped over the rubble behind him, she asked, "Why don't you change back? You'd fit so much better then."

"No one is likely to bother us while I'm in my dragon form," Audun said as he started down the corridor. "I find that people tend to get out of my way when I'm like this."

"I don't blame them," said Francis. "They'd get squashed if they didn't."

Audun followed his nose to a door set off by itself at the very end. He stepped aside as Francis muttered something and pressed the palms of his hands against the door. It opened easily and Francis hurried in. Annie

148

followed, but Audun stayed in the corridor and peered inside.

The room they had given Zoë was much larger and more elegant than Annie's. The bed was hung with brocade, while cushioned chairs faced each other across a thick rug. They found Zoë standing by a table holding a blood-filled chalice.

"Don't drink that!" Francis said, snatching it away. "It's probably drugged."

"I'm sure you're right," said Zoë. "I never drink blood if I have a choice, but I'm so thirsty and this smells delicious."

Francis took the acorn from his pocket. He poked his finger inside and pulled out the glistening tip of a unicorn's horn dangling from a golden chain. Holding the chain above the chalice, he dipped the piece of horn into the blood. The blood fizzled and bubbles popped. When he pulled the unicorn horn out, the blood looked the same as it had before. "You can drink it now if you want to," he said, holding it out to her. "It was drugged, but it isn't anymore."

Zoë shook her head and pushed it away. "No thanks," she said. "I'll turn into a bat and forage for insects again as soon as we're well away from this place, which may not be for a while yet."

"Why can't we leave right now?" asked Annie.

"Not until we find out why Maganen was lying," Zoë replied. "Did you see the way he looked above me and couldn't meet my eyes when he said that my parents left as soon as they learned that the duke wasn't here? My father told me that vampires do that when they're lying. I don't trust either Reynard or his friend to tell the truth about anything."

"You're right," said Audun. "You shouldn't. I can smell your father in this room. He's been here very recently. I can't smell your mother, though. At least not in this room. I did smell her out in the corridor when we first entered the castle."

"I didn't know that dragons had such a great sense of smell," said Annie.

"I once tracked Millie from the Icy North all the way to Greater Greensward by scent alone," Audun said.

"I don't understand why my parents would be separated like that," said Zoë. "They always stay together when they go visiting. I don't like this at all!"

"Do you think your parents are still here?" asked Annie.

"I don't know," Zoë replied. "But I'm going to find out! Audun, please see if you can find my father's scent anywhere else."

Audun stepped away from the doorway and sniffed. The others followed him to the stairwell. They were going down the stairs when Annie said to Francis, "You said that harpies guard the area around the castle during the day. What about inside the castle?"

"They don't need guards inside," Francis replied.

"Once the castle is locked down, there's no way anyone can get in or out except by air, and the harpies have that handled."

"Why would Zoë's parents want to stay here at all, and especially when the duke isn't around?"

"They wouldn't," Francis said. When Annie glanced at him again, his mouth was set in a grim line.

Audun stopped to sniff again, and the silence reminded Annie of the day she'd spent in her parents' castle, awake while everyone else was sleeping. It was a memory she didn't want to relive, so she was relieved when he started walking again. He led the way down the next flight of stairs as well, taking them to the door where he had stopped to sniff before.

"Huh," he said. "Now I smell both of your parents, Zoë. They must have brought your father down the stairs while we were talking to Reynard."

Zoë tried the door and it wasn't locked. When Audun saw that it opened onto a stairwell, he groaned. "This is going to be a tight fit."

"It's dark down there," Francis said as he peered into the stairwell. "I can take care of that!" Shaping a ball with his hands, he created a witches' light, which dimmed and went out as soon as Annie moved closer.

"Why don't I go first and send the lights ahead of me. Annie, you follow Zoë, and Audun can go last," he told her. "We won't have any light if you walk near me, Annie."

They waited while Francis made more balls of light, then concentrated on their footing as they headed down. Audun grunted as he descended the stairs, scraping the walls with his scales so that stone dust filled the air, making the others cough.

When they reached another level, Annie and Zoë waited in the dark while Francis and Audun went to investigate. They were gone only a few minutes before they were back with the lights bobbing above Francis's head. "Is he here?" Zoë asked when they drew closer.

"No, and that's a good thing," said Francis.

"The duke's dungeon is on this level and it's not a good place to be," Audun explained as they started down another flight of stairs.

The second flight was far longer than the first. They weren't even halfway down when Annie smelled something acrid. The smell grew stronger the lower they went, until the stench was overwhelming. By the time they reached the bottom of the stairs, Annie's head was pounding.

"What is this place?" she asked as Francis created more witches' lights and set them loose above them.

"A cavern, from the looks of it," said Zoë. "And if I'm not mistaken, the ceiling is covered with bats. Do you still smell my parents, Audun?"

"I can't smell anything besides the bat mess on the floor," Audun told her. "We'll have to try something else to locate them now."

"My dragon scale will work," Francis said as he took it out of the acorn. "It couldn't tell me where Garrid and Li'l had been, like Audun's sniffer could, but it can tell us where they are now. Be quiet, everyone. We don't want to wake those bats."

"This is their home and they feel safe here. Aside from a natural disaster, the only thing that will wake them is the sunset," said Zoë.

The others crowded around Francis to see the dragon scale. "Lead us to Zoë's mother," he said. The scale flashed red as they walked to the middle of the cave, then turned blue no matter which way he faced.

Zoë shook her head. "I don't understand. Mother should be right here."

"Look up," Audun said. "I think we found her."

Everyone tilted their heads back. It was hard to see in the shadowed upper reaches of the cave, but when Francis waved his hand, the witches' lights began to rise ever so slowly. They could see the bats better now. Even more importantly, they could see the cage suspended from the ceiling. When Francis pointed the scale straight up, it flashed bright red.

"They stuck my mother in a cage?" Zoë cried. "How dare they!"

"I wouldn't put anything past Reynard," said Annie. "How are we going to get her down?"

"I could fly up there," Audun suggested.

"Now *that* would probably wake the bats," said

153

Zoë. "I'll go up and let her out. Stay here, I'll be right back."

Having seen a vampire float outside her window in Treecrest, Annie knew that they could fly in human form, but she was still surprised when Zoë drifted up to the cage. Because it was still too dark to see much so high up, she expected to see Li'l when Zoë came back down. When the vampire princess landed beside them, however, she was alone and looked upset.

"She's in there all right, but I can't open the cage door or get the cage down from the ceiling," Zoë told them. "Someone must have used some very complicated magic to secure it. I feel just awful! Mother was huddled on the floor crying when I got there and looked so hopeful when she saw me. When I couldn't do anything, she started crying all over again."

"I can help from down here," Francis told her. "Emma taught me the spell that she used to untie a string from your mother's leg when they were both locked in a witch's cottage. It's a simple spell, but it's very useful. Audun, if I can touch you while you're a dragon, it should amplify my spell enough to overcome any vampire magic."

They all looked up at the cage as Francis cleared his throat and said:

Unlatch, unlock, undo, untie,
In the twinkling of an eye.

Open ye lock,
Lift ye latch,
Remove ye block,
Release ye catch.

A deep rumble made the cage sway. The door opened as it fell and Li'l fluttered out even before Audun snatched the cage out of the air and set it on the ground. At the same time a door set into the cave wall opened, Annie's braid came undone, and the sash around her waist came untied. Francis looked surprised when the belt holding up his scabbard fell to the ground, but Zoë was too focused on her mother to notice that her necklace had come undone and fallen into the neckline of her tunic.

"Wow!" said Francis. "That really worked! Thanks, Audun."

Li'l fluttered to her daughter's shoulder. "Thank you so much, Francis!" she told her son-in-law. "I was afraid I was going to spend the rest of my life in that cage. Have you found Garrid yet? Is he all right?"

"We're still looking for him," said Zoë. "We think he's down here somewhere."

"He is," Li'l told her. "I saw some guards carry him into that room just a little while ago. Follow me." Fluttering her wings, she rose off Zoë's shoulder and headed for the door that the spell had opened.

"Why can I understand your mother?" Annie asked Zoë as they ran to the door.

"Emma cast a spell on her years ago so Li'l can talk like a human," said Zoë. "Everyone can understand her now."

Zoë followed her mother into the room and stopped, forcing Annie to peer around her. Hewn from rock, the room was no more than a small cell with chains attached to the wall. The chains dangled unused and unneeded; the handsome man lying on the floor looked as if he would never rise again. Blond with chiseled features and broad shoulders, he was better looking than any of the other vampires Annie had met, despite his terrible pallor. She could see a striking resemblance to Zoë.

With a cry, Zoë sank onto her knees beside her father. "Is he still breathing?" Francis asked, hurrying to her side.

Zoë pressed her cheek to his chest and held up her hand for everyone to be silent. "I can hear his heartbeat," she said after a while. "But it's very faint. His breathing is shallow, too."

"He was poisoned," Audun said from the doorway. "I can smell it on him."

Li'l landed on her husband's chest and stamped her tiny feet. "Wake up, Garrid!" she cried. "You know how much I love you. Don't leave me. You're supposed to outlive me by centuries!"

When Garrid didn't stir, Zoë shook his shoulder, saying, "Father! Can you hear me?"

"I could nip him if you'd like," Audun said. "That always works on Millie."

"You will not bite my father!" Zoë told him.

"I'd offer to try a spell, but I don't think my magic would work on him," said Francis.

Zoë shook her head. "Don't bother. Your spells never work on me, so I doubt they could help him."

Annie jumped when a horrific screech broke the silence of the cavern. Zoë's head whipped around so she was facing the door. A moment later, she and Francis exclaimed, "Harpies!" at the same time.

"My spell must have opened everything in the castle," Francis said as Zoë got to her feet. "I bet the harpies saw the open doors and came inside. We have to go and we have to do it now."

"I can carry your father," said Audun, "but we'll have to fight our way past the harpies."

"No, we won't," Annie told him. "Not while I have this." Reaching into the pouch she wore on her hip, she took out the postcard for Greater Greensward. The others drew closer to touch Annie while the harpies flooded the cavern behind them. Then Annie placed one hand on Garrid's chest and the other on the center of the postcard. A moment later, they were gone.

CHAPTER 14

"QUICK, WE HAVE to get him in the castle," Zoë told the guards standing by the drawbridge.

The men hurried over and worked together to pick up Garrid's limp body and carry him into the castle.

"Get Princess Emma and my wife," Audun told other guards as the four friends hurried through the courtyard. He paused long enough to turn human again before dashing up the stairs.

The men carried Garrid into a bedroom and laid him on the bed. His face was pure white and even his lips were pale. Zoë stood beside the bed with silent tears trickling down her cheeks while Li'l nuzzled his neck, begging him to wake up. Minutes later, Emma and Eadric came running into the room with Millie and Audun close behind.

"What's wrong?" Emma cried. "What happened to Garrid?"

"The vampires at Highcliff poisoned him, but we don't know why," said Francis.

Li'l propped herself up on a wing to look at him. "I know why," she said. "I was there when they did it. Reynard and his friend had just come back from a trip when Garrid and I showed up. Reynard said that his uncle was dead and that he was in charge. When Garrid asked what happened, Reynard told him a ridiculous story about traveling to the other side of the world and getting into a fight with humans. They told him that the duke had been the first to die and they had fled, leaving him behind. Reynard said they'd come back when they did because Highcliff needed someone to rule over it. When Garrid ordered them to return to this faraway land and retrieve the duke's body, Reynard got all agitated. Garrid was still talking when Reynard took out a little box and blew some stinky powder in my honey's face. When he turned all white and funny looking and fell out of his chair, I started shouting and flying around. One of those terrible vampires grabbed me and stuck me in that awful cage and hung me in the cave where their relatives sleep."

"When you say 'stinky powder,' do you mean it actually smelled bad?" asked Emma.

"It does!" said Li'l. "I can still smell it on his face."

Audun nodded. "I can smell it, too. It's very faint, but it reminds me of the way the harpies smelled when they entered the cavern."

159

"You saw harpies?" Emma said, shuddering.

"That's who protects the sky around Highcliff Castle during the day," Annie explained. "We think they came into the castle when your spell opened all the doors."

"My spell?" said Emma. "You're going to have to tell me everything that happened very soon, but first we have to help Garrid. If the duke was dealing with harpies, that powder might well be something that they made. I wish I could help, but I don't know any way to cure something like that. We'll need a healer who knows about such things. Audun, could you go fetch Millie's doctor and explain that it's an emergency? We need his help right away."

"I'll go with you," Millie told her husband. "I know where to find him."

As Audun and Millie ran from the room, Annie turned to Emma and said, "Do you have a healer who actually knows about this kind of thing? When my father was sick with the creeping blue, we had to travel a long way to find someone who could help."

"Oh, yes," said Emma. "We have a wonderful witch doctor who only just moved to the area. A friend of ours convinced him to move here."

"Really?" Annie replied.

She was about to ask more questions when Zoë said, "We should take off Father's shoes and make him comfortable. Who knows how long he'll have to lie here like this. I don't want him to wake with a crick in his neck."

"The doctor should be here soon," Emma said, even as she helped Zoë. "Audun can fly very fast when he wants to."

They were covering Garrid with a blanket when they heard a commotion in the corridor. Annie peeked out and saw a small furry animal skipping beside a short man whose long, dark hair was tied back in a ponytail. His clothes were baggy and looked as if they didn't quite fit him. "Ting-Tang!" she cried, and ran to meet him. "No wonder Zoë and Emma were so confident that their doctor could help Garrid! I hoped I'd see you again someday. I just didn't know it would be so soon."

The witch doctor set down the drums he was carrying so he could give her a hug. "Princess Annie! I thought you lived in Treecrest."

"I do, or at least I did. Liam and I have moved back to Dorinocco to get ready for his coronation. I came to Greater Greensward to ask for help with vampires."

"Vampires? And I hear you all brought me a patient who is sick from harpy poison. My, you do live an interesting life," said Ting-Tang.

Annie laughed. "Sometimes it's a little too interesting. Your patient is in here. We can catch up later," she said, leading him into the room.

Everyone moved aside as Ting-Tang approached the

bed. After looking at Garrid's pale face, smelling his breath, and listening to his heart, he said, "I'll need a few things for a potion if I'm going to help this poor man. Get me freshly collected honey made from clover, some lavender, violet blossoms, rose petals, thyme, sweet spring water, bread, butter, and pickles."

Emma looked confused. "Does it matter what kind of pickles?"

Ting-Tang shook his head. "No, Chee Chee isn't picky. He's developed a real taste for pickles and loves them all."

"The pickles are for your monkey?" asked Annie.

"Yup, and the bread and butter is for me," said Ting-Tang. "We haven't eaten yet today and we're both hungry."

"What about the honey?" Emma asked.

"That's for the potion, of course," Ting-Tang told her. "Why do you ask?"

Emma sighed. "Never mind. Sweet spring water won't be a problem. The sweetest spring water around feeds the castle well."

"I'll get the water and the bread, butter, and pickles," offered Millie.

"Francis, why don't you and I get everything else?" said Annie. "Zoë should stay here with her father."

"I'll go with you," Audun told her. "Sick people make me uncomfortable."

"There are roses and lavender in the garden just outside the moat," Francis said as he started out the door. "We can get those first."

He took them out of the castle, stopping only long enough to get a jar for the honey and a basket to carry everything. After crossing the drawbridge, he took them to a lovely garden facing the road. While Annie collected rose petals, Francis found the lavender. Audun was watching them when he said, "Have you found the thyme?"

"Time for what?" Francis asked.

"For the potion," said Audun.

Francis looked confused. "I don't understand. We're spending our time getting the ingredients for the potion right now," he said, plucking one last sprig of lavender.

"I think he means t-h-y-m-e," Annie said. "You know, the herb Cook uses in some of her dishes, and the maids strew on the floor with the rushes to make the great hall smell better?"

Francis nodded. "Right! Next stop—kitchen garden."

"You really didn't need me along, did you?" Audun asked as they started walking again.

"Not yet," said Francis. "But we still might."

They found the thyme easily enough in the kitchen garden. Because Ting-Tang hadn't told them how much they needed, they took a lot, covering the lavender and rose petals until the basket was half full. "Now what?" Annie asked. "All that's left on Ting-Tang's list are the honey and the violets."

"I know where to find some violets, but they won't be in bloom," said Audun. When Francis gave him a funny look, Audun shrugged. "Violets are Millie's favorite flower and I pick her a bouquet when I can."

"Where is this place?" asked Annie.

"Near the treehouse," said Audun. "Follow me."

Annie enjoyed the walk around the moat where water lilies floated and dragonflies hovered. When they passed the field set up for jousting practice, she liked seeing the knights taking turns charging their horses at the quintain. Even so, she was beginning to wonder how much farther they would have to walk when they finally reached a copse of trees where a ladder led up to a treehouse.

"That was Grassina and Chartreuse's treehouse when they were little girls," said Francis. "It fell into disrepair when the family curse changed my grandmother, but Mother fixed it up when she had me. I played in it a lot when I was little. It's bigger inside than it looks."

They found plenty of the heart-shaped violet leaves growing around the base of the trees, but none of the plants were blooming. "Don't worry," Francis told his friends. "I know what to do. Annie, would you mind standing back there?" He pointed beyond the treehouse to a spot where she could stand without affecting his magic.

After Annie had walked far enough, Francis knelt in the midst of the plants and came up with a spell:

Violets are pretty,
Violets are sweet,
New blooms would be a wonder,
New blooms would be a treat.

Your blooming season's over,
But bloom now anyway.
Your flowers are what's needed
To help a friend today.

Although Annie was too far away to see the buds form, she could see the flowers unfurling. When they had all bloomed, she came back and helped Francis and Audun pick them. "Isn't Garrid your father-in-law and not just a friend?" she asked Francis.

"Yes, but that didn't fit," Francis replied. "I've found that when I make up spells, the right rhythm gives it a little more power. What counted was the blooming, not who it was for."

"Here, this should be enough," Audun said, placing a few more violets in the basket. "If there are any left over after Ting-Tang takes what he needs, I can give the rest to Millie."

"And now for the honey," Annie announced.

"That might be a little harder," Francis told her. "My dragon scale can help me find the hive, but we'll have to get the honey ourselves."

Audun sighed. "Let me guess—that's where I come in."

"If you wouldn't mind?" Francis said with a grin.

"Oh, I'll do it," Audun replied. "I just hate getting my scales sticky."

Annie took the basket while Francis looked at his dragon scale. "Show me where I can find a beehive filled with clover honey," he announced. The scale flashed blue until he turned back the way they had come. With the scale leading them, they returned to the castle, then headed down the road to a hayfield rich with clover. A sycamore tree stood in the hedgerow running along the back of the field. As they drew closer, Annie saw bees swarming around a hive partway up the tree.

Annie and Francis turned to look at Audun. "Get that jar ready; I'll be right back," he said.

Audun turned into a dragon even as he approached the tree. Planting his hind feet firmly on the ground, he reared up so that his head was level with the hive. Bees buzzed around him angrily as he used his talons to break a hole in the hive and dig out a chunk of honeycomb. Annie could hear the faint *ping* as the bees tried to sting him, but only managed to break their stingers against his scales. Batting at the bees hovering around his face, he sat back on his haunches and turned to Annie. When she held up the jar, he shoved the comb inside.

"That's everything!" Annie said as she set the jar in the basket.

A few of the bees were still hovering around Audun, so he remained a dragon as they started back. Finally, when they still wouldn't leave him alone, he blew a tiny puff of his poison gas at them. The bees immediately turned and zigzagged away, flying erratically. "I've never made bees nauseous before," he said as he turned back into his human self. "Now I feel bad."

Annie grinned. She'd never imagined that a powerful dragon could be so soft-hearted.

❧

When Annie and her friends returned to the room where Garrid was still lying unconscious, they found Ting-Tang seated at a table with a mortar and pestle, a pitcher of water, and a half-filled mug of cider in front of him. Annie set the basket on the table, nearly bumping into Chee Chee, who was sitting on the floor holding an empty pickle jar and licking his fingers.

"Good!" Ting-Tang declared. "Now we can get started."

Setting aside the honey, he sorted through the basket's contents, then took a pinch of each item and put it in the mortar. After using the pestle to grind them

167

together, he added a dollop of honey, a splash of pure spring water, and a shake of something from a pouch he'd brought with him. When the ingredients in the mortar began to bubble and froth, Ting-Tang carried it over to Garrid. "Prop him up," he told Zoë and Emma. As soon as they'd raised Garrid's head, he poured the contents of the mortar into the vampire prince's mouth.

Everyone pressed closer to see what happened. When nothing did, Zoë exclaimed, "It's not working!"

"It will," Ting-Tang said as he moved the table out of the way.

"How long do we have to wait?" asked Emma.

"Not long," Ting-Tang replied. He turned to look at everyone in the room. "You might want to leave for the next part. It's going to get loud in here." Fetching his drums from the corner of the room, he set them on the floor by the bed. Annie noticed that there were two sets; one big and one little.

"I would leave now if I were you," Annie told Emma and Zoë, who had lingered beside Garrid. "If Ting-Tang says it's going to be loud, it's going to be *really* loud."

They all hurried from the room as Ting-Tang and Chee Chee sat down in front of the drum sets. Li'l perched on Zoë's shoulder just outside the door. Annie thought it looked as if they were holding their breath.

As soon as Ting-Tang hit his drum, the monkey gave

his own set two firm raps. And then they started pounding. "Walla walla bing," Ting-Tang shouted, followed by an extra loud *Bang!* on his drums.

Chee Chee started screeching. He pounded his drums as hard and fast as he could, his little monkey paws flying up and down.

Even from outside the room, the noise was loud. Everyone watching through the doorway stuck their fingers in their ears, but they didn't stop watching. Annie gasped when she thought she saw Garrid's finger twitch. When he sat up and looked around, Ting-Tang finished his drumming with a flourish.

"Father, are you all right?" Zoë cried, running into the room.

"Garrid!" Li'l shouted, and landed on the blanket covering him.

"I'm fine," he said, rubbing his temples. "Except for a pounding headache from that drumming. It was so loud!"

"It had to be loud enough to wake the dead," Ting-Tang said as he got to his feet. "Although you weren't dead, you were close to it. That potion brought you back part of the way, but we needed the drumming to do the rest. You'll be fine now."

"Thank you so much, Ting-Tang!" Zoë cried. "You were wonderful."

The witch doctor shrugged. "All in a day's work," he

said. "I like helping people. Plus, Chee Chee and I got to practice our drumming!"

"I have to ask," Annie said as Ting-Tang picked up his drums. "Whatever happened with Liam's brother, Clarence? He was supposed to stay in the jungle with you and be your assistant. Did he come back, too?"

"No," Ting-Tang said, shaking his head. "As far as I know, he's still in the jungle. He never did like being my assistant and he ran off with a girl from the jungle a few days after you left. I heard through the jungle vine that he ended up with that tribe where you found me and seemed quite content. Sorry I couldn't keep him with me longer. I know how important it was to you and Prince Liam."

"We don't really care where he is, as long as he doesn't return to Dorinocco," said Annie.

After walking Ting-Tang and Chee Chee to the door, Annie returned to her friends. Zoë was telling her father about everything they had gone through while looking for him.

"But you didn't say why you were looking for me in the first place," he finally said.

"I think Annie should tell you that part," Zoë told him.

"It was because of the postcards," said Annie. "People have been buying magic postcards at the Magic Marketplace and using them to come to Treecrest, my parents' kingdom. First there were witches, then a lot of different kinds of people. We thought everyone had gone until we discovered the vampires. They started biting people in the castle and they wouldn't leave. I came to Greater Greensward to ask for help. Zoë and Francis went back with me and they helped us get the vampires out of the castle, but they refuse to leave Treecrest."

"I said we should come ask you to help," said Zoë. "But you were gone and no one knew exactly where you were, so we started retracing your route."

"Do you think you could come to Treecrest and help us?" asked Annie. "Please?"

"Of course," Garrid said. "It sounds as if this is my problem as well. If Reynard left his uncle there, dead or not, this whole thing might be a ploy of his to gain control over Highcliff. It's about time the duke learns what's going on at home. And if any vampires refuse to return, I might have to teach them a lesson of my own."

Chapter 15

"Francis and I are going to Treecrest with Father and Annie," said Zoë. "Anyone else want to go?"

"I will," Emma replied. "I might be able to help."

"I'd go if I could," Eadric said, "but I promised I'd go to Soggy Molvinia today. They're having a problem with werewolves and their traps aren't working."

"I'm too tired to go," Li'l told them. "I was so worried about Garrid that I didn't get a wink of sleep in the horrible cage."

"I wish I could, but I don't feel well," said Millie. "I don't think I can go anywhere today."

Audun looked concerned when he said, "I'm staying here with Millie. I've already been away too much lately."

"You have postcards for Treecrest and Greater Greensward, don't you, Millie?" asked Zoë. "Would you please let me borrow them? I'll give them back as soon as we get home."

"Come upstairs with me and I'll give them to you," Millie replied. "Good-bye, everyone, and good luck. Please come see me as soon as you get back. I want to hear all about what happens."

They were ready to go less than an hour later. Garrid was covered from head to toe, wearing a long, hooded cape and gloves. "He can't stay in the sun for long, even dressed like this," Zoë warned Annie.

"Is this what vampires wear when they visit the Magic Marketplace?" Annie asked.

"It is," said Emma. "I've seen a few vampires at the market over the years. Although a lot of people go there dressed in unusual clothes, vampires still stand out like sore thumbs. You never see more than one or two at a time and they don't stay long."

"Vampires go out in the daylight only if it's absolutely necessary," Zoë explained. "I think this is one of those times. Father, you stand next to me and hold on to my arm. Francis, you stand over here."

While Francis and Garrid held on to Zoë, Emma held Annie's hand and watched with great interest while the younger princess touched the center of the postcard.

"It's just like going to the Magic Marketplace!" Emma cried when they arrived in Treecrest a moment later. "What will they think of next?"

It was almost dusk, and Annie wanted everyone to get inside as quickly as possible. She smiled when

Emma exclaimed how beautiful the castle looked, but as soon as Zoë, Francis, and Garrid walked up, she hurried them toward the drawbridge.

Guards were already raising the drawbridge when Annie took her guests into the castle. She was walking down the corridor when Liam stepped out of the great hall and swept her up into a bear hug. He kissed her while Garrid and Emma watched, amused.

"I assume that this is your husband," Emma said as Liam set Annie back on her feet.

Annie laughed. "Yes, this is Liam, prince of Dorinocco and soon to be king. Liam, this is Zoë's father, Prince Garrid, and Millie's mother, Princess Emma. They've both agreed to help us with the vampires."

"I'm honored to meet you and grateful for any help you can give us," said Liam.

Squidge's cat friend, Scarface, sauntered down the corridor. Suddenly he stopped and sniffed. Spotting Garrid, the cat hissed, turned tail, and ran back the way he'd come. A moment later, Annie's parents appeared in the great hall doorway.

"Annie, you're back!" Queen Karolina called. She and the king hurried to greet their daughter and the new arrivals.

Annie made the introductions all over again, but she noticed that Liam kept glancing toward the door leading outside. When Captain Sterling approached, Liam finally said, "The captain and I have to go on our

174

rounds. We check every door before it's fully dark out, just to make sure that they're all closed and locked. If you'll excuse us?"

"They do it every night," Queen Karolina said as the two men joined a group of waiting guards. "I don't know if they feel it's absolutely necessary or if they're doing it to assure us that we're safe, but it does calm my nerves. Thank you so much for letting Liam stay here with us. He's been wonderful since you left and knows just what to do."

Servants were lighting torches in the corridor and the great hall when Squidge ran up to hug Annie around her knees. "Scarface told me that you were here," he said. "He told me that you have a vampire with you, too. Is it that guy? Why is he all covered up like that?"

"That's Zoë's father. He's come to help us," said Annie.

"Did they tell you about the vampire parties?" Squidge asked her. "They hold them in the courtyard and they're really loud."

"Who is this?" Emma said, crouching down to get a better look at Squidge. "I've never seen anyone like you before."

Squidge stepped away from Annie and stood as straight and tall as he could manage. "I'm a sprite," he said. "And proud of it. Who are you?"

"I'm Princess Emeralda of Greater Greensward, a

kingdom very far from here. I'm also the Green Witch and I hope to help with your vampire problem."

"It's not my vampire problem," Squidge declared. "I discovered something new and I'm having a great time. I was spying on their party the night after Annie left and this dopey-looking guy with greasy hair and terrible teeth grabbed me and tried to bite my neck. He'd barely touched me with his chompers when he dropped me and started to howl. He got all slobbery and a minute later his big pointy teeth fell out! It looks like sprite blood is too sweet for those guys to handle."

"Are you all right?" Annie asked him.

"Me? Oh, yeah! Right as rain," Squidge said, and pulled back his collar to show her his neck. "He didn't even leave a mark. Anyway, every night I try to get more vampires to bite me. They can't resist me 'cause I'm so very tasty. I heard one say that I smell like vampire candy. Making them lose their teeth is more fun than sticking cherries on porcupines. I'm up to sixteen vampires now."

Garrid hadn't really seemed interested in Squidge at first, but hearing this he looked horrified. He studied the sprite without moving any closer. After one sniff, he nodded and said, "I must admit, you do smell delicious. I can understand why a vampire might find you irresistible."

"See! Just like I told you," Squidge crowed. "And if I

176

get sweaty, they like me even better. I must smell *really* good then!"

"What happens if a vampire's fangs fall out?" Emma asked the vampire prince.

"They cannot feed from the source and must drink stored blood or they will die," Garrid said, looking grim.

"Are there many sprites in this part of the world?" asked Emma.

"Lots and lots!" Squidge said with glee. "I have seventeen brothers and eighteen sisters and more cousins than Scarface has fleas."

Loud music started in the courtyard and everyone turned toward the door. "That sounds like the kind of music that vampires play at their parties," Garrid told the others.

"They've had a party in the courtyard every night since you left, Annie, and there isn't anything we can do about it," said the queen. "When I heard it the first night they were here, I thought it was lovely, but I hate it now."

"Even the raised drawbridge doesn't stop them," the king declared. "Once the sun goes down, those monsters fly over the wall and do whatever they please. I think they have parties just outside our door so they can rub our helplessness in our faces."

"I believe it's time that I see for myself what's going

on," Garrid said. "Zoë, why don't you go with me and point out the vampires who attacked you? After I deal with the duke, they deserve my particular attention."

"I'd be happy to," said Zoë. When Francis started walking with them, she shook her head. "You need to stay here for now. We're not going to fight with them unless they force us to."

Francis pulled her into his arms. "I just want to keep you safe."

"She'll be safe," Garrid assured him. "I won't let them touch her. Lock the door behind us and don't let anyone in unless you're certain it's Zoë or me. If all goes well, this shouldn't take very long."

Annie had no intention of letting her friends handle her kingdom's problems without her. As soon as Zoë and the vampire prince walked out the door, she ran upstairs and found a maid to help her into her suit of armor. When she returned to the corridor outside the great hall, her parents were gone, but Liam and Captain Sterling were there with the guards and they were all wearing their armor. Francis wore his golden armor as he paced by the door near where Emma was talking quietly to Squidge. The vampires' music was playing just as loudly as before.

"I'm going out there," Annie announced. "And no one is going to stop me."

"We don't want to stop you," said Francis. "We've been waiting for you. We're going out, too."

"The captain and I are going first in case the vampires are waiting to ambush us as soon as we walk out," Liam said as he pulled his sword from its scabbard. "Ready?"

When everyone acknowledged that they were, Liam opened the door. The steps were clear, so he and his men proceeded down into the courtyard while Annie, Francis, and Emma followed them, taking cover behind a wagon. One of the guards who had stayed in the corridor closed the door and locked it.

"There's Garrid," said Francis. "Zoë's there, too."

Zoë saw them at the same moment and came running to talk to them. "I told you to stay inside!" she said, frowning.

"Did you really think I would when I knew that you were in danger?" Francis asked her.

Zoë sighed. "I suppose it was too much to ask. There hasn't been much danger, though. They're more interested in the stale blood they're drinking than they are in us. Father and I have been listening in on their conversations while I pointed out the troublemakers. He's been marking them and, well, you'll see."

They all turned to watch as Garrid approached another vampire who didn't notice when the vampire prince touched his hand. The spot he'd touched glowed red for a moment, then faded as the prince walked away.

"I see the duke is still alive," said Annie.

"Indeed," Zoë replied. "I was pretty sure Reynard was lying."

The Duke of Highcliff was talking to some other vampires when Garrid approached him. Curious to hear what they said, Zoë and her friends crept closer.

"Your Highness!" the duke said, sounding pleased when he saw the prince. "When did you arrive?"

"A short while ago," said Garrid. "What I want to know is why you're here."

The duke shrugged. "My nephew suggested it. He purchased some magic postcards at the Magic Marketplace and brought me and some of my friends here to see a different part of the world."

"And yet you're still here," said Garrid.

"We were going to stay only a few days," the duke admitted, "but the humans turned on us and threw us out. It became a matter of honor. We couldn't just leave after that."

"Was it Reynard's suggestion that you stay even after you were asked to leave?" Garrid said. "And that you fight the humans who own this castle? I've known you for many years and you've always been an honorable man. I would never have expected this of you. You've put far too much trust in the word of your brother's son. Did you know that your nephew returned to Highcliff without you? He's telling everyone that you're dead. Reynard and his friend have taken over your castle."

"He did what?" the duke said, no longer sounding affable. "I haven't seen him for a few days. He told me that he and his friend were going off to explore the countryside and would be back soon. That scoundrel! Please excuse me, Your Highness, but it's time I return home to deal with Reynard!"

"Make sure that he's punished appropriately," said Garrid. "Because if you don't, I will. Reynard poisoned me with harpy dust, locked up my wife, and tried to keep my daughter prisoner. When we got away, harpies were overrunning your castle. I doubt very much that your nephew can handle it."

The duke was furious when he took a postcard from his pocket. "By your leave, Your Highness," he said. Three other vampires crowded close to him and they all disappeared at once.

"As for the rest of you," Prince Garrid said in a ringing voice loud enough to hear throughout the courtyard, "I marked those of you who attacked my daughter, a royal princess. My symbol will stay with you for three years, showing everyone that you are traitors to the royal family. Should you do only good within those three years, the mark will fade until it disappears. Should you continue in your disrespect to my family or your fellow vampires, the mark will remain and you will be ostracized from the company of all vampires."

The partiers turned to look at one another. When

181

any of them spotted a vampire wearing the prince's mark, they backed away as if he were contagious. One by one, the unmarked vampires took out their postcards and left Treecrest until only the vampires who bore Garrid's mark remained.

"You can't do this just because of your daughter," shouted one of the marked vampires. "She's not even a full-blood."

"I don't care how powerful they are, half-bloods don't have the right to tell us what to do!" shouted another vampire.

"Yet she is my daughter and I am your prince," Garrid declared. "You owe fealty to me and respect to everyone in my family."

"I don't deserve your mark," a vampire cried. "None of us do. Yet now we have nothing to lose!"

As if at a silent signal, the vampires unsheathed their swords and rushed Garrid and Zoë. Garrid waved his arm and the vampires flew back as if a giant had swatted them. They were on their feet a moment later, hurling themselves at the prince and Zoë again.

When Francis, Liam, and Captain Sterling ran to defend the vampire prince, Emma put her hand on Annie's arm, keeping her there. "I was afraid this might happen," said Emma. "I think we need reinforcements who are more effective against vampires than a mere sword. This spell should do it."

Friends of Squidge and family, too,
Little sprites, I call on you.
Vampires came and will not leave.
They taste our blood and they believe
That they have every right to stay,
And plague us in their loathsome way.
We need your help, we need it now.
Please help us make them go somehow.

Annie flinched when lightning flashed and thunder boomed even though the sky was clear. She remembered that Emma wasn't just the Green Witch, the most powerful witch in Greater Greensward; she was also a dragon when she wanted to be, and so had dragon magic. When the wind started to blow, Annie had a good idea what might be coming next.

The vampires were trying to overwhelm Garrid and his defenders when the first sprites arrived, carried on winds that they controlled. Then Squidge was there, telling them what to do, and they ran toward the vampires, laughing with glee. Emma held on to Annie, anchoring them both as wind blew from every direction, buffeting them and almost knocking them down. More and more sprites came until the courtyard seemed to be overrun.

At first the vampires didn't appear to notice what was happening, but as the urge to bite the sprites became overwhelming, and one vampire after another lost their fangs, those attacking the prince came to understand their peril. The fangless vampires were the first to use their postcards to leave, crying out in anguish and despair. With their numbers diminished, the rest followed soon after.

"That was amazing!" Annie said, and hugged Emma.

Emma laughed and said, "I'm just glad it worked. I'm beginning to think that there aren't any vampires in your part of the world because of the sprites. They may be adorable, but they're deadly to vampires, a creature that everyone else fears."

"Where did all those sprites come from?" Liam asked as he joined Annie.

"Emma used her magic to bring them here," Annie told him.

"It was a great way to end the fighting, except for one thing," he said as a trio of giggling sprites rode by on Scarface's back. "What are your parents going to do with all these sprites?"

"I hadn't thought of that," said Annie. "I was more worried about all the witches and vampires who still have postcards. What's to stop them from coming back someday?"

"I don't think they will," Emma told her. "Especially not after word gets around that you can take away magic and that the sprites can make vampires lose their fangs."

"Emma, that was an inspired idea!" Zoë cried as she joined her friends.

Her father was watching the sprites playing on the wagon when he said. "It was indeed, although I must admit, I'm a tiny bit afraid of those sprites myself." When Squidge strolled up with Bumpo the hedgehog, the vampire prince stepped out of their way.

"Who would have guessed that we had our own solution with us all along?" said Annie.

"Uh, now that all these sprites are here, how long do you think they plan to stay?" asked Liam.

"Feed them now and they'll be gone before morning," said Squidge. "They all have homes and jobs that need them."

"I'm curious," said Emma. "What do sprites like to eat?"

"Breakfast pastries!" Squidge said, clapping his hands in delight. "And lots of them!"

CHAPTER 16

"I CAN'T BELIEVE that you can eat more pastries!" Annie declared. "Not after you gorged on them last night."

Squidge and one of his younger sisters, an adorable, tiny girl named Posy, were seated cross-legged on the table just past Annie's trencher. All the other sprites had departed during the night after eating the vast number of breakfast pastries that Cook and her helpers had stayed up to make.

Squidge patted his rounded belly and sighed. "You can never have too much of a good thing, and Cook's pastries aren't just good, they're great! We have to get the recipe to take to your cook in Dorinocco. I could eat these every day."

"You're still going back with us?" asked Liam.

Squidge nodded. "Sure am. You need me! That reminds me, Your Majesty, do you think you might be able to hire my sister?" he asked, turning to Queen Karolina. Despite their late night, both the king and queen had gotten up to say good-bye to Annie and Liam, who planned to return to Dorinocco that day. "Posy needs a job and it seems to me that you can use a sprite here. She's good with animals and can keep all yours in line."

"We don't have very many animals in the castle," said the queen. "Just a few hounds and a cat or two. And the horses, of course."

"Actually, you have seven cats and ten dogs, including the ones that live in the stable. And then there are the chickens and doves and mice and rats and roaches and flies and—" Posy began.

The queen shuddered. "I see your point."

"And if any vampires come back, I can offer to let them bite me and chase them away," Posy told her. "I was really good at it last night."

"It might not be a bad idea to have you here," said the king. "Just in case."

"My biggest fear is that more people might buy the postcards and the same thing might happen all over again," Annie said.

"I thought about that as well," Garrid said from his seat beside King Halbert. "I propose that we visit the Magic Marketplace and talk to the vendor selling the postcards. I'm sure we can come to some sort of arrangement."

187

"You mean ask them to stop selling the cards for Treecrest?" asked Annie.

"Precisely!" the vampire prince replied.

When he smiled, Annie couldn't help but wonder what he really had in mind.

"Millie lent me all the postcards she bought when she went there with you," said Zoë. "Including one of the Magic Marketplace. I could take you if you'd like to go."

"That would be wonderful!" Annie told her. "The sooner we can get them to stop selling the Treecrest postcards, the sooner we can stop worrying."

૪૭

Annie, Zoë, and Garrid weren't the only ones to go to the Magic Marketplace. Francis went because Zoë was going, Emma went because she needed to buy someone a present, and Liam wanted to see what else was for sale. "You still want a singing sword, don't you?" said Annie.

"Well, yeah! Have you seen the sword Francis bought? I want a sword just like Torrin," Liam said, his eyes shining. "Plus, I didn't really look around at the other stalls. Who knows what else I might find?"

The moment they arrived, they all headed straight for the postcard stand. It was easy to spot because it had the biggest crowd around it. All sorts of people were there, from witches and wizards to sylphs, full-sized fairies, nymphs, a well-mannered ogre, and at least two vampires covered in capes and hoods. Annie and Liam stayed close to Emma, who pushed through the crowd toward the green-haired witch manning the money box. Somehow, Garrid managed to be there ahead of them. Even dressed in an enveloping cape and hood, the vampire prince looked both mysterious and intimidating, whereas the other vampires just looked creepy.

"You have no right to sell postcards for a kingdom that doesn't want visitors," Garrid was telling the witch when Annie arrived.

"No one from that kingdom has complained to me about it," said the witch.

"We are now," said Annie. "I'm Princess Annabelle from Treecrest and we want the postcards for our kingdom removed from your stall immediately."

The witch sneered at Annie. "We don't always get what we want, dearie. If I stop selling yours, I'd have to stop selling cards for all the others who complained. That's not going to happen."

"What if we buy all the Treecrest cards you have in stock and you guarantee that you won't make or sell any more?" asked Emma.

"I don't know," the witch said. "Treecrest cards have become awfully popular. You'd have to pay three times the standard rate for each card."

"I got all the Treecrest cards on the stand," Francis said, waving them in the air as he joined his friends. "There were four."

"There's four there, and twenty-two that I haven't set out yet," the witch said with a gleam in her eye.

A wizard waiting to buy postcards was studying one for Treecrest. When Emma noticed this, she said, "We'll also want all the cards that people are holding in their hands."

The wizard glared at Emma. "I'm not giving this up! I'm using this card right after lunch."

"No, you're not," Emma said, and turned back to the witch. "Either I get every Treecrest postcard in the Magic Marketplace right now, or I'll make sure that none of your cards work again. They'll be nothing but pretty pictures of faraway places that no one will ever visit."

"You can't do that. I'd be ruined!" cried the green-haired witch. "Everyone would want their money back." She gestured and two large dogs walked up, stiff-legged and growling.

"I'm sure you're right," Emma told her. "It's your choice. Give up the Treecrest cards, or lose your business."

The witch laughed nervously. "I shouldn't even listen to you. This is a magic-free zone. No one can use unauthorized magic here. There's a dampening spell on the entire market that prevents it."

The dogs drew closer, their hackles raised.

"No ordinary witch can," said Emma. "But then, I'm

not ordinary. I doubt the dampening spell is any match for me."

The witch gasped when Emma started to change. Everyone backed away as she grew, turning into a beautiful emerald-green dragon over twenty feet long. The two dogs guarding the stand ran off with their tails between their legs.

"A dragon!" someone shouted.

"There's a dragon in the marketplace!" cried another voice.

"Is that even allowed?"

"Who's going to make it leave? I'm not, are you?"

"Fine!" the witch cried, cowering behind her table. "Take the Treecrest cards!"

"Three times the standard rate?" Emma said as she started to turn back. With a flick of her wrist, all the Treecrest cards that people had already selected flew out of their hands to form a pile on the table. "Now, where are the twenty-two cards that you mentioned?"

The witch bent down to fumble in some boxes under the table. When she stood up, she added the cards to the others.

After Francis counted the cards, Emma paid the woman. "And you'll guarantee that you'll never make any more Treecrest postcards?"

"Oh, I promise," the woman said, holding up her hand.

"Good!" said Garrid. "Because if any more unwanted guests use a postcard to visit Treecrest, I'll find out where you live and send my friends and relatives there for a nice, long visit."

The woman turned ashen when he pushed back his hood enough that she could see his face. "Aren't you the vampire prince?" she asked, her voice a harsh whisper.

"I am," he said. "You might want to recall all the Treecrest postcards you sold before we showed up today. No uninvited postcard visitors, remember?"

The green-haired witch nodded, saying, "I'll do my very best!"

"Now," said Emma, "what am I going to do with all these cards?"

"I'll carry them for you," said Francis, and took out his acorn. Liam seemed especially interested to see the entire stack disappear inside.

When the table was cleared, Emma turned to Annie and said, "Would you like to look around?"

Annie nodded. "I'd love to."

"Francis and I are going in this direction," Liam said, and the two took off into the crowd.

"If we're finished here, I'm going home," Garrid told Annie. "The market is too sunny for me."

"Oh, of course!" Annie exclaimed. "Thank you so much for everything you've done."

The vampire prince shrugged. "Apparently, it was

192

my mess to clean up. Thank you for helping Zoë. Her mother and I are forever in your debt."

Zoë hugged her father and was watching him go when Emma asked Annie, "Did you want to look for something in particular?"

"A coronation gift for Liam. We're supposed to be crowned when we return home."

"Then we'll start with this aisle," said Zoë, and led the way.

"What do people usually give for coronation gifts?" Annie asked as they started walking.

"I don't really know," said Emma. "I've never gone to a coronation."

"What do you think he'd like?" Zoë asked. "Something unusual, something fun, or something useful?"

"I'm not sure," Annie replied. "I was hoping I'd know when I saw it."

They were walking past a stand where a parrot was preening in front of a full-length mirror when Zoë said, "How about a magic mirror?"

The parrot swiveled its head to look at Annie. "Magic mirror! Magic mirror!" it squawked.

"Liam doesn't really need one," Annie said, even as she studied the assortment at the stall. There were small mirrors she could hold in her hand and tall mirrors that rested on the floor and could show an entire person. Some mirrors had fancy gilded frames while

193

others were framed in old, cracked wood. Annie particularly liked a simple, silver-edged one that fit on a table.

"Everyone needs a magic mirror!" exclaimed the parrot. "You can ask it all sorts of questions like who's the fairest in the land, where does the milkmaid go in the middle of the night, or where is a traveling relative right this very minute?"

"I hadn't thought of that!" said Annie. "We could ask the mirror where Clarence is now that Ting-Tang is gone."

The parrot stepped away from the mirror and pointed at it with one wingtip. "Go ahead. Ask it."

Annie shrugged. "All right. Mirror, where is Prince Clarence of Dorinocco right this very minute?"

The reflection of Annie and the marketplace dissolved into a sea of swirling blue. An image seemed to float closer and soon she could make out Clarence dancing around a fire with a group of wildly gesturing people. The trees behind him were just like the ones she'd seen when she and Liam had gone with Audun to rescue Ting-Tang.

"Good!" Annie declared. "I'll have to tell Liam."

"So, which mirror would you like to purchase?" asked the parrot.

"Like I said before, we don't need one," said Annie. "We already have a magic mirror at home. It just never

occurred to me that we could use it to check up on Clarence."

The parrot bristled and clacked its beak. "If you're not buying, don't waste my time by pretending that you are!" As another young woman approached, the parrot strutted over to her screeching, "Magic mirror! Magic mirror!"

"He was rude!" Zoë said as they walked away.

"The merchants here often are if you're not buying anything," said Emma. "Didn't Liam say that he wants a singing sword? We could look at those."

Annie laughed. "I'm sure he's choosing one right now. Oh, look! That man is selling magic acorns like Francis's. Liam would love that!"

Annie hurried to the stall where a picture showed a flood of objects pouring into a capless acorn. "Could I see one of your acorns, please?" she asked the man behind the table.

"Sorry, miss, but I just sold my last one," the man replied. "However, I do have a lovely watermelon suitable for holding entire buildings."

"No, thank you," Annie said with a sigh. "The acorn would have been perfect."

They walked on, pausing now and then to look at something, but nothing seemed quite right to Annie. She liked the magic instruments that played themselves, but wasn't sure that Liam would. The magic horseshoes that never needed replacing were a possibility, but she thought she could do better. After a while she narrowed her choices down to a pillow that guaranteed a restful sleep or a water jug that poured endless amounts of clean, fresh water.

"Which will it be?" Zoë finally asked. "I'm sure either one is a good choice."

"The pillow, I suppose," said Annie. "Liam hasn't been sleeping well lately, and he can be so grumpy when he isn't rested."

When Annie returned to the stall to buy the pillow, Zoë wandered off in search of Liam and Francis. Annie and Emma were waiting for them when they overheard a group of people talking. "Did you hear that a dragon was in the market earlier?" one of the people said.

"Really?" said another. "I wish I'd seen that! I would have stolen one of its scales to make my magic stronger."

"I would have killed it and sold off the body parts. Imagine what you could get for the heart and lungs."

"You couldn't kill a dragon! You can't even kill a chicken for supper!"

"Well, I would have tried."

"That's awful!" Annie told Emma as they walked away. "Why would people say such things?"

"Because they want to sound brave when they really aren't," said Emma. "The ones who brag about it aren't usually the ones who would actually try. If they do try

it's because they want to prove something or their friends have goaded them into it. People like that always sound brave until they meet you face-to-face. Real dragon hunters are much more discreet, and that's what makes them dangerous. You don't always know when that kind of person is coming after you."

"Have you ever faced a dragon hunter?" Annie asked her.

"A few times, but then, I don't usually turn into a dragon in public places like this," Emma replied. "I've heard lots of stories, though, and none of them end well for the humans. It's very hard to kill a dragon because of their physical toughness and their magic. Usually when you hear that someone killed a dragon, it's because the poor creature was sick and dying anyway."

"Annie, what did you buy?" Liam called as he walked toward them down the aisle between the stalls.

Annie glanced at the basket she'd bought to carry the pillow. "A surprise," she said when she looked up.

Liam grinned. "I love surprises when they come from the Magic Marketplace."

Although Liam wasn't carrying anything in his hands, she guessed that Francis could be carrying it for him in his acorn. "Did you buy anything?" she asked.

"That's for me to know and you to find out when I'm ready to tell you," Liam said, looking pleased with himself.

The postcards didn't work anywhere in the market-place except the area around the fountain, so they all turned and started that way. Francis joined Zoë and Emma while Annie walked with Liam, who seemed to be in a very good mood. After studying his face for a moment, Annie said, "Promise you won't be mad?"

"That depends," said Liam. "Mad about what?"

"I know you weren't happy that I invited all the fairies from Treecrest and Dorinocco to the corona-tion, but I've thought of a lot more people I want to invite. I'm sure you won't really mind once you hear who I'm talking about. Our coronation is going to be the best one ever!"

CHAPTER 17

BECAUSE ALL THE PEOPLE they'd invited needed time to get there, the coronation didn't take place for another two weeks. By then, the floors were all washed and strewn with fresh rushes, the tapestries and banners had been taken down, beaten, and rehung, the chalices polished, the gears of the drawbridge oiled, and even the display of small wooden animals that Liam had carved were dusted and rearranged. When Annie told Squidge that all the sprites who had helped to chase away the vampires were invited to the celebration, he contacted them via fairy messenger right away. A whole squadron of sprites descended on the castle, helping with the cleaning and polishing, chasing down the cats, dogs, and vermin to wash them, and generally getting in the way whenever possible. Not wanting to be outdone, the fairies of Treecrest and Dorinocco arrived two days early to help decorate the castle, festooning the great hall with flowers and placing songbirds on every window ledge.

King Montague didn't know what to make of all the activity, and took to his bed for a day. But after a fairy visited him, taking him tea and tiny cakes, he decided that he liked it and installed himself in the great hall, telling everyone that he was in charge. Edda sat with him, watching the hustle and bustle with great interest. The fairies were kind enough to humor the king and let him decide which flowers went where and whether they should bring butterflies or hummingbirds to flutter around the flowers. They were overjoyed when he suggested they have both.

When the royal guests began to arrive, the old king was still the center of attention. The fairies used magic to move his throne to the dais, along with new ones for Annie and Liam. After King Montague sampled all the tasty confections that Cook was making, the king's gout started bothering him again, so he sat on the dais with his foot propped up, watching all the activity. Edda lay down beside him.

The morning of the ceremony, King Montague was back on his throne when Annie and Liam walked up. Edda stood and nudged Annie, asking to be petted. Annie was happy to oblige.

"I don't think the castle has ever been this clean or this beautiful," the king told them. "And all the people!

I've never seen so many here, and they're still arriving! It's a sign of how popular you two are. A very good sign, indeed."

"Annie is the popular one," Liam told him. "None of this would be happening if it weren't for her."

"You have friends here, too, Liam," said Annie. "Captain Sterling and Francis have both become good friends of yours. And Millie said that Audun was very unhappy until Ting-Tang announced that she was able to make the trip. He really wanted to come to the coronation, but he didn't want to leave her behind."

"True," said Liam. "But just about everyone else is here because of you."

"I think Liam is right," the king said, nodding. "You are a treasure, Annie! I'm so glad you didn't fall asleep in the Treecrest castle like Liam's mother had planned. You and Liam are just right for each other. Much better than my wife and me. It's such a relief that she's settled in to life on the witches' island so I don't have to worry about her nasty tricks. Tell me, who is that beautiful woman dressed in blue who just walked in the door?"

Annie glanced at the door and smiled. The only woman wearing blue was an older, white-haired witch whom Annie and Liam had met in Greater Greensward.

"That's Azuria, the Blue Witch," said Liam.

"I've heard that she just broke up with her farmer boyfriend," Annie added. "It would be nice if you talked to her for a few minutes."

"It would be my pleasure!" the king replied.

Edda barked when Squidge bounded up the steps carrying a well-groomed mouse. "The king and queen of Treecrest just arrived," the sprite announced. "And I spotted a bunch of other royal-looking people I don't recognize coming down the road."

"Then we should go outside to greet them," Annie told Liam.

"I'm going, too!" Squidge said, and jumped on Edda's back. The troll dog shook herself, but the sprite held on, chuckling when she started to walk.

By the time they reached the steps to the courtyard, Annie's parents were descending from a beautiful new carriage that she had never seen before. The entire carriage was covered with silver and the doors were emblazoned with flowers made from semiprecious gems. "Hello, darling!" said her mother. "Don't you just love the carriage? It's your coronation gift from your father and me. We commissioned a family of dwarves to make it."

"The dwarves used their magic to make the stones stay on. They'll never come off, not even if you try to remove them with a dagger," said King Halbert. "I tried it just to see if their magic worked and it does."

"Thank you so much!" Annie cried. "It's lovely. I'll make sure I don't touch the stones. I'd hate it if they fell off because of me. Perhaps I'll ask Francis and Audun to reinforce the spell."

Queen Karolina glanced up at the roof and called, "Posy, we're here. Come see Squidge."

"She rode on the roof all the way from Treecrest?" asked Annie.

Her mother shrugged. "She insisted on it. She said she likes the view and the feel of the wind on her face."

The little sprite girl popped up from behind some ornate curlicues on the roof, yawning. "Sorry, I fell asleep. I always sleep during long carriage rides."

"Come down!" her brother called from Edda's back. "I have lots to show you. Everyone else is here already."

"We're the last ones to arrive?" asked Queen Karolina.

"Not at all," Annie said. "He meant all the other sprites are here. They've been very helpful in their own way. Just watch where you step. They do tend to get underfoot."

"I'm sure they do," said the king. "But I must admit, Posy has been a big help. Some vampires showed up one night with postcards in their hands and Posy chased them off. We haven't see any since."

"I'm glad to hear that!" Annie declared.

The sound of more arrivals clattering over the drawbridge drew everyone's eyes and suddenly there was a flood of royalty as one carriage after another vied for space in the courtyard. Annie's aunt and uncle, Queen Theodora and King Daneel, were there with their son, Prince Ainsley, and his wife, Ella. Their carriage had scarcely moved out of the way when two more rolled up carrying Annie's sister, Gwendolyn, and brother-in-law, Beldegard, his parents, King Berwick and Queen Nara, and his twin sisters, Willa and Tyne. When King Dormander of Scorios and his daughter Mertice arrived, Annie was thrilled that they had come. (She still thought of Mertice as Lilah, the girl who had hidden herself at Snow White's court disguised as a servant.) When Prince Andreas rode up, he took one look at Mertice and started following her around like a puppy.

Princess Snow White, her father, King Archibald, and her intended, Prince Maitland, were next. Then Prince Emilio rode up on horseback with his two children, Tomas and Clara, and his cousin, Prince Cozwald. As soon as Willa and Tyne saw the younger children, they took them from Prince Emilio and ran off with them to explore the castle.

"We'll keep an eye on the children," Squidge declared, and he and Posy took off after them astride Edda.

"I don't know if that's a good thing or not," Annie whispered to Liam.

Silver sparkles in the air announced that the fairy

Moonbeam and her husband, Selbert Dunlop, were there. Ella was thrilled to see her and hustled the couple over to meet her in-laws. The most dramatic arrival, however, was when Emma, Eadric, Grassina, Haywood, Francis, Zoë, Millie, Ting-Tang, Garrid, and Li'l rode in on a flotilla of magic carpets with Audun, their dragon escort. Everyone gasped and got out of their way as the carpets settled to the ground and Audun landed beside them.

"I know I agreed not to let people see me as a dragon in Treecrest, but they know about vampires now," Audun told Annie and Liam once he'd changed back. "I figured that it wouldn't hurt for people to see that dragons are real, and not necessarily scary."

"It's all right," said Annie. "So many things are changing. The people need to know about the good as well as the bad."

Squidge rode up on Tyne's shoulder. "You're not wearing that for the ceremony, are you?" the twin asked, looking Annie over.

The little sprite pinched the girl's ear. "Be polite! These are my humans," he told her before turning to Annie and Liam. "It's time for you two to get ready or you'll hold everyone up!"

"Sorry!" Annie said with a laugh. "I promise we'll be fast."

Annie's and Liam's clothes were already laid out when they walked into their bedchamber. While Annie dressed in her best gown of pale blue silk, Liam donned his uniform in matching blue. They went downstairs hand in hand. When they reached the corridor leading to the great hall, fairies fluttered around them and sprites scattered flower petals on the floor in front of them. Annie sighed as they reached the doorway and the music began to play. She had Liam at her side and her family and friends were there. As far as she was concerned, it couldn't be more perfect.

Annie and Liam were walking down the center aisle when she saw King Montague waiting on the dais at the far end of the hall. He looked resplendent in his cloth of gold over-tunic and his gold crown on his head. Annie couldn't understand why the air seemed to be sparkling above him until she realized that the fairies were sprinkling him with gold dust.

Still holding hands, Annie and Liam stepped onto the dais and stood facing King Montague. Annie was listening to the king talk about passing the crown on to the person he trusted the most when suddenly there was a disturbance at the edge of the hall. The sprites had climbed the pillars to get better views, and some of them were batting at the butterflies flying from flower to flower. A sprite with bright pink hair had reached too far and fallen off the column, landing on the head of a courtier below. The woman shrieked in surprise, and cried out even louder when the sprite

 206

leaned over and looked her square in the eye. Annie couldn't help but laugh as the sprite jumped from the woman's head back onto the column to return to his former perch.

King Montague didn't seem to notice and kept talking about the responsibility of the person who sits on the throne as the crowd turned back to listen. He was winding up his speech when, out of the corner of her eye, Annie saw one of the twins tweak the wing of a nearby full-size fairy. The people around the fairy gasped, anticipating some sort of reprisal, but she just smiled at the twin and waved at her as if they were already friends.

Annie turned back to face King Montague when Liam nudged her. Husband and wife knelt as the old king lifted the crown from his own head and set it on Liam's. Then, taking a new, fairy-made crown from a satin pillow, he set it on Annie's head, making her the new queen of Dorinocco.

Annie looked up and smiled. The crown was as light and delicate as a dandelion puff and it rang with tiny bells every time she moved. Although the fairies had asked her what kind of crown she wanted, she hadn't seen it before this. It was better than what she'd anticipated and she already knew she loved it.

Everyone cheered when Annie, Liam, and the old king turned to face the hall. Annie's heart swelled as

she gazed out over everyone she cared about and saw how happy they all looked. After Liam sat down on the center throne with Annie on one side and his father on the other, people approached the dais with gifts. There were so many presents that Annie was overwhelmed until Snow White volunteered to keep track of everything for her. Aside from the carriage that Annie's parents had already given them, they received jewelry and horses from Andreas, Cozwald, and her royal relatives, a painting of his children from Emilio, a blue parrot that was fluent in seven languages from Azuria, a suit of armor that would actually fit Annie from the Treecrest guards, and their very own potted moonflower from Moonbeam and Selbert.

The very best gifts came from her Greater Greensward friends.

"I thought you could use these," Emma said, handing Annie the stack of Treecrest postcards. "You may keep them or distribute them as you see fit. I also made you some for Dorinocco so you can go back and forth more easily."

"That's wonderful!" Annie cried. "Thank you so much!"

"I got you that water pitcher you were eyeing," Zoë said, handing her the pitcher from the Magic Marketplace. "I know how much you liked it."

"Oh, I did!" said Annie. "The decision was really hard. Thank you!"

"We're giving you each a dragon scale," Millie said as Audun handed them over. "To help you find things."

"And I thought you might like a little music," Garrid said, unveiling a magic harp.

"My present is actually for King Montague," Ting-Tang told them. "I noticed that he has gout, so I picked a few things in your forest and prepared a potion in your kitchen. Have him take one sip every day for five days and he'll be as good as new."

"That's fantastic!" Annie exclaimed as Montague beamed.

After the last gift was revealed and Annie and Liam had thanked the last person individually, Annie declared to everyone there, "Thank you all so much! We're delighted that you were able to join us on this special day, and we thank you all for your thoughtful gifts."

Everyone cheered them once again. When they turned away, they discovered that the fairies had set up the tables and benches, and food was already waiting for them. People were taking their seats when Moonbeam came up to Annie and Liam.

"Squidge told me that he no longer wants to work in the Moonflower Glade," said Moonbeam. "He says he wants to stay here with you instead. According to him, you two really need him to keep your lives in order. He says that you are forever having problems that he can solve. I told him that if it was all right with you, it was fine with me. It is all right with you, isn't it?"

Annie glanced at Liam and laughed. "I guess so," she said. "He already feels like part of the family. Are you sure you won't need him?"

Moonbeam nodded. "I'm positive. He's made it plain that he doesn't like Selbert. Sometimes it's a real struggle to keep that little squirt from playing nasty tricks on my sweetie. Selbert still hasn't gotten over finding a family of skunks in his clothing trunk. Good luck with Squidge. He can be a real help some days, and a real challenge others."

"We've already noticed that!" Liam declared.

"Annie, I have to say that the day your parents had me cast a spell to keep magic from ever touching you, I thought they were making a big mistake. I was wrong, though. You've actually turned out to be quite wonderful. Who would have thought it?"

As Moonbeam walked away, Annie turned to Liam. "I got you a pillow at the Magic Marketplace that's guaranteed to give you a restful sleep."

"I could really use that!" Liam told her. "Thank you. And I got you an acorn like the one Francis has. You wouldn't believe how much that thing can hold."

"So you're the person who bought the last one!" Annie said, smiling. "I know those acorns can hold a lot, which is why I wanted to get one for you. It's funny, though. People were thinking about what I would like when they bought the magical gifts, but they're really all your presents. Most of them won't work when I touch them."

"I guess people tend to forget that," said Liam. "I think they mostly remember how sweet and brave you are."

"Did you get yourself a singing sword?" Annie asked him.

Liam shook his head. "I remembered what happened when I looked at them last time. I don't really need a sword that loses its magic when you're around because I never want to be separated from you again."

A group of people at a nearby table laughed and Annie turned toward them. "Look at that," she said, gazing down at the variety of guests seated side by side at the tables. "Witches and fairies seated with sprites and vampires and humans and they all seem to be having a marvelous time."

"The world is changing," said Liam. "Those postcards made a big difference and we can't put things back the way they were before, even if we wanted to."

"I know," said Annie. "All we can do is make sure that the people we love can handle the change and don't lose sight of what's important."

"Like family and friends?" said Liam.

Annie nodded. "I was going to say the ones you love most. Congratulations, King Liam. I just know that you are going to be a wonderful ruler."

"As are you, Queen Annabelle," Liam said with a

smile. "I'm the luckiest king around, and Dorinocco is the luckiest kingdom to have a queen like you. Who would have thought that growing up without magic would make you the most wonderful princess of all?"